"Stay down!"

Troy yelled, pulling a gun Kate didn't realize he was carrying from the back of his pants as she lay there on the floor just watching.

Someone was shooting...at her. Why? From where?

What in the hell was going on?

Troy moved behind the kitchen island in a squatting position facing the direction from where the bullet had come. Whoever was shooting must have been posted somewhere behind her house. There were several houses that were at the same or higher level than hers, so the shooter could have been anywhere.

She was going to need to invest in blackout blinds, something that no one could see through.

Be in the moment. She had to stay in the moment. She couldn't dissociate now.

She belly crawled toward the living room, making sure that she stayed behind cover as she moved. Beside the doorway, by the pantry, was a Glock 43X she had bought and stashed for an occasion just like this one, one she never thought would actually happen.

Thank you to all those who have helped make this book and this series come to life. This has been a fun series to create and see grow and change over time. I hope that these characters and their stories are just as real to you as they are to me.

A special shout-out to my editors at Harlequin and my agent, Jill Marsal. Your constant and unwavering faith in me is humbling and greatly appreciated.

Also, thank you to Jennifer (who keeps me fed with homemade cookies), Kristin, Clare, Melanie, Herb, Penny, Joe, Mike and Troy. These folks are my behind-the-scenes helpers who help me research, write, edit and even beta read these books at (sometimes) very short notice. To say it takes a village is an understatement!

A LOADED QUESTION

DANICA WINTERS

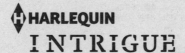

This book is dedicated to all those folks who spend far too many
holidays behind a computer, rifle, or going dark. Thanks for
making this world a safer place. You are the true heroes.

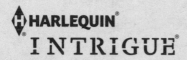

ISBN-13: 978-1-335-40156-4

Recycling programs
for this product may
not exist in your area.

A Loaded Question

Copyright © 2021 by Danica Winters

All rights reserved. No part of this book may be used or reproduced in
any manner whatsoever without written permission except in the case of
brief quotations embodied in critical articles and reviews.

This is a work of fiction. Names, characters, places and incidents
are either the product of the author's imagination or are used fictitiously.
Any resemblance to actual persons, living or dead, businesses,
companies, events or locales is entirely coincidental.

This edition published by arrangement with Harlequin Books S.A.

For questions and comments about the quality of this book,
please contact us at CustomerService@Harlequin.com.

Harlequin Enterprises ULC
22 Adelaide St. West, 40th Floor
Toronto, Ontario M5H 4E3, Canada
www.Harlequin.com

Printed in U.S.A.

Danica Winters is a multiple-award-winning, bestselling author who writes books that grip readers with their ability to drive emotion through suspense and occasionally a touch of magic. When she's not working, she can be found in the wilds of Montana, testing her patience while she tries to hone her skills at various crafts—quilting, pottery and painting are not her areas of expertise. She believes the cup is neither half-full nor half-empty, but it better be filled with wine. Visit her website at danicawinters.net.

Books by Danica Winters

Harlequin Intrigue

STEALTH: Shadow Team

A Loaded Question

Stealth

Hidden Truth
In His Sights
Her Assassin For Hire
Protective Operation

Mystery Christmas

Ms. Calculation
Mr. Serious
Mr. Taken
Ms. Demeanor

Smoke and Ashes
Dust Up with the Detective
Wild Montana

Visit the Author Profile page at Harlequin.com.

CAST OF CHARACTERS

Troy Spade—Troy is a broken man after his fellow military contractor and girlfriend is killed in front of him. Coming back to the States, he and his siblings become part of a special operations team, STEALTH Surveillance, a group that has been hired to scope out any possible weaknesses in the ConFlux security walls.

Kate Scot—An agent for the FBI, she finds herself in a situation dripping with intrigue when her father's company comes under fire just a few blocks from her office. When Troy walks into her life, what was already complicated suddenly takes on a series of whole new twists as she is forced to answer for her parents' possible crimes.

Solomon Scot—The CEO of ConFlux, a man with as many skeletons in his closets as he has dollars in the bank.

Deborah Scot—The former CFO of ConFlux, the woman who stands to become the largest stockholder if everything goes her way.

Mike Spade—Troy's brother and a fellow military contractor from the STEALTH Surveillance team.

Zoey Martin—Leader of the STEALTH military contractor group. As smart as she is cold and calculating, she is the linchpin that keeps everything running.

Agent Peahen—Kate's coworker from within the Bureau, a man who seems hell-bent on taking Kate down professionally.

Rockwood—A corporation with ties to a variety of illegal and nefarious endeavors, including the theft of military weapon-grade secrets from within the USA.

ConFlux—A company hired to help engineer and manufacture military-grade weapon systems for the different branches of the US military. Their contracts are highly sought after and extremely lucrative, and prove quite the target for their enemies to try to sabotage or steal.

STEALTH—A military contracting group hired for a variety of jobs. Within the organization, Zoey Martin has created the Surveillance team made up of the six Spade siblings to learn more about the Rockwood organization and their affiliates.

Prologue

Nothing is ever easy... The biggest understatement of the millennia. There was nothing worse than being imperfectly human.

Troy Spade's mission was supposed to be relatively simple, just a protective security detail to take their medium-risk VIP to the border checkpoint, hand their strap hanger off to the next team, and then they were to head back to the tactical operations center. Intense, but normal. If they didn't screw things up, they would be done within a couple of hours, debriefed and back to playing *Halo* on the Xbox.

Tiff glanced over at him, sending him a smile as she drove. He both loved and hated her for the sexy look. This wasn't the time or the place to bring up all the things they meant to one another. And yet, with that sex-laced smile, all he could think about was running his fingers down her soft, perfect skin as they lay in her bed. This morning, when they had woken up, she had given him a similar smile, except thoroughly sated, well loved and blissful. He was hers and she was his. In that single action, she and their love were everything he needed.

She was his happy place, and he could think of nothing better than spending his days in the constant conflicts that came with war-torn nations and private contracting, and his nights in the peace of her embrace. He had it all.

He took in a breath. Underneath the scent of sand, sweat and gun oil he could still make out the scent of her on him. He loved the way she naturally smelled of woman, and when she wore perfume, it only intensified his need to hold her in his arms once again.

Dammit, Troy. Come back to reality, he thought, checking himself. *This. This right here is why being with her isn't a good idea.*

He couldn't have love. Love was a weakness. Love would compromise their objectivity. Love could lead to only one thing—failure. And failure wasn't an option. In their line of work, failure was death.

A stray piece of hair had slipped out from under her helmet and was threatening to fall into her eyes as she drove. He was tempted to reach over and fix it for her, but that was the last damn thing he could do. He peered into the back seat where their gunners were seated, watching out the windows and looking for any possible threats.

If they even guessed that there was something between him and Tiff, Troy's butt would be on the line, and one, if not both him and Tiff, would be on the next plane back to the States. Then the honeymoon would really be over and he would have to go back to some dead-end job where he struggled to make ends meet.

Not an option.

As the detail team leader, they followed behind the VIP, driving offset as they cruised to the objective. He glanced down at his watch. Ten more minutes, if the roads remained clear, and they would be at the Albanian border. Ten more and they would be headed back. Within the hour they would be safe... *She* would be safe. And maybe, for at least a few hours, he could finally relax. Well, at least relax as much as any person could who was hunkered down in enemy territory, where they stuck out and were about as welcome as a saddle sore.

Oh, the things he would do for money.

The car in front of them wove to the right as they moved to the left in their trademark zigzag pattern. Ahead of them, on the opposite side of the road, a small white car pulled over and stopped. The gunner behind and to his left steadied a bead on the sedan's driver though the car had gotten out of the convoy's path. If random vehicles didn't get out of the way, their convoy would have no qualms in chewing them up and spitting them out.

Just as they were about to pass by the white car, the driver flipped a U-turn, and tires squealing on the hot blacktop, the car charged in the other direction.

Troy turned to Tiffany and opened his mouth, about to issue a warning about the odd behavior, when the up-armored vehicle they were riding in quaked. In slow motion, the black hood of their Suburban launched upward as the violent boom rattled him to his core.

He'd never heard a sound quite like it, the tearing of metal, his friends' screams swirled with his own, and it all mixed with the thrashing of his heart. It meant only one thing…

We're hit.

The world twisted around him as he tried to get his bearings. Their SUV careened through the air, flipping hood over bumper as they took the full impact of the explosively formed penetrator… It had to be an EFP—it was the only thing that could have blown them up like this. Or it could have been an IED. But that wouldn't have hit this hard or done this much damage. Maybe it was an RPG, but again, it wouldn't have screwed them up like this. Definitely an EFP.

The irony didn't escape him that even though they had yet to land, he was arguing with himself about what they had just experienced. Dissociation at its best. Maybe dying wouldn't be so bad after all—at least he wasn't swirling that cognitive drain. An odd sense of peace drifted through him.

Tiffany's cry pulled him back to reality…to the terror that filled him, the smell of burning rubber and the acrid smoke that filled the air, and to the pain radiating up from his legs. He started to move to see if he even had legs; as he did, he spotted the blood. The crimson liquid was spattered across the inside of the snowflake-patterned broken glass of the front windshield.

It was supposed to be bulletproof.

Definitely an EFP.

A droplet of blood slipped over the glass, toward the ground flashing by them.

There was a strangled cry, the sound a soft mew, like that of the breathless.

Tiff.

He looked over. She stared at him with a wide-eyed, terrified look upon her face. Her mouth was open, the strangled sound still twisting from her lips. The steering wheel she had been holding was gone, as was everything below her shoulder. At the center of her chest, impaled in her core, was a long jagged piece of metal that looked like it had once belonged to the engine block.

Following his gaze, she looked down at the shrapnel in her chest and then back up at him. Her wail stopped as the last bits of breath rattled from her body.

The car slammed down, hitting the asphalt with the screech and shudder of metal meeting stone. There was a shatter of glass as it broke away and exploded through the air and hit his face. It felt like the cold, icy graupel that came on a cold winter day, except each impact was followed by the hot ooze of rising blood.

Tiff's gaze met his and she smiled through her

pain. The light in her eyes, the spark that drew him like a moth, dimmed, and he watched as her life slipped away.

This was it. He was in hell. Everything he had ever done had caught up to him. Here. Now.

It had to be hell… Only in hell would he be forced to watch the woman he loved die…and not be able to do a damn thing to save her.

Chapter One

Everyone was fighting a battle—whether it be in the Siberian tundra, the Afghanistan deserts or in the territory of the heart. And just like all battles, there could be only one victor…and, regardless of conqueror or conquered, all lost something.

Kate Scot had won many battles, and yet had gone on to lose what she held dear more times than she cared to admit. Most recently, that loss came in the form of her apartment and dog—now both in the hands of her ex-boyfriend. She would really miss that dog; she'd had Max since he was just eight weeks old.

But she didn't hate her ex for kicking her to the curb. Far from it. Given her line of work, it was only a matter of time before he figured out that he was too good for her and it was time to move on to someone else—someone who could dote on and fall over him in ways she never could. Not to mention her inability to completely open up with him.

He had deserved better. And she definitely needed

to be alone for a while, and out of the game that was dating.

Dating was for people who had a vacant space in their heart, a space that could be unlocked and given freely—again, something she'd never been capable of doing, or perhaps even willing to do.

She held no doubts that it was the warrior mentality and her training that kept her feelings from ever entering the equation. As a woman in her field, she was constantly falling under the scrutiny of those around her—they pressed her for weakness, both consciously and subconsciously, regularly checking her boundaries and her capabilities. For that reason, above all, she had to be the best of the best within her team.

And it was this thirst for recognition and push to prove herself that had resulted in her receiving the email that now nearly pulsed with its red "immediate attention required" subject line. The sender, Aaron Peahen, was from the Billings office, and though they were from the same state, there was little love between them. Peahen had a penchant for bringing out the worst in her, and from the times they had worked on joint assignments—the last of which had ended with them throwing insults under their breath at one another—she didn't bring the best out in him, either.

He appeared to be so old-school that he operated as if having women in the agency was some kind of nuisance the male agents had to grin and bear in order to make the public happy. He would never, no matter how well respected she was, accept that she was just as valuable a team member as he.

No doubt, he had sent her this case to set her up for failure, or send her on some wild-goose chase.

Just like warm milk, regardless of what Peahen sent her, she doubted it got better with age.

She clicked on the offending flag. As she read the email, she could hear Peahen's deep, rasping smoker's voice like he was standing over her shoulder instead of six hours away across the state.

Agent Scot,
It has come to my attention that you have materials associated with a case I'm currently working. Do you have time for a phone call? Better yet, I would appreciate you just sending me everything pertinent to case #HJ1085-090.

Your prompt response would be appreciated, but I know this can be a problem for you. Regardless, I need this within seventy-two hours, or I will be forced to contact your superiors regarding the matter.
Agent Peahen

Agent Peacock was more like it. He was all show and no teeth.

And there she had thought, for nearly a moment, that she didn't absolutely despise her fellow agent. Wrong. What a jerk. He couldn't treat everyone else this way or he would have been out on his butt and pounding the pavement long ago... Nope, this kind of derision seemed to be aimed straight at her center mass.

Well, he could fire away.

She clicked on her files, opening up the requested information. It was last time-stamped nearly five years ago, and as she scrolled through her file, she could barely recall the information about a bank robbery she had investigated when she had been new to the area.

The investigation hadn't gone anywhere, and within a month of her initial investigation, it was allowed to go to the recesses of her computer files to catch dust.

Until now, and Agent Peacock wanted to take the case under his wing.

Rage bubbled up from her core. No doubt Agent Peacock had some kind of plan to grandstand and show what a great agent he was by playing off some failed case of hers.

She let an audible grumble slip past her lips.

"You okay over there, K?" Agent Hunt asked, looking up from his computer for a brief moment. He was paying only half attention, but she appreciated that he had even seemed to notice that something was amiss.

Before she could even answer, Hunt had turned back to his work on the screen.

That, that right there was one of her favorite

things about their team. They all cared about each other, but not enough to pry or ask too many stupid questions. More, they never found the need to do any more talking than absolutely necessary to get the job done. With it came little miscommunication, hurt feelings or stepping on each other's toes.

She pressed back from the desk, her chair rolling over the hard plastic on the floor, making a crushing sound.

"Eating sunflower seeds again?" Agent Hunt asked. "That is a disgusting habit, you know."

Of course, he would be keyed in on her one little quirk. She should have been more careful to keep her mess from hitting the floor.

"We all have something we do to pacify ourselves. Don't get me started about your gum popping." She smiled at him, hoping he would realize she wasn't about to say anything about his tics.

Hunt chuckled as she stood up, grabbed her suit jacket and slipped it over her arms. "Where you going?"

"Out."

In all honesty, she didn't know. The only thing she knew was that she could not continue to sit there and stare at Peahen's email for another second. Sure, she could've just sent him the information he wanted and gotten him out of her hair, but she'd never been the type to give in that easily. If he wanted to be a jerk, two could play that game.

She pulled up the file on her phone, and waiting

for it to load, she looked over at Agent Hunt. "You want to go for a ride? Are you working on something?"

Agent Hunt shrugged. "As luck would have it, I'm currently beating level 2421 on *Candy Crush*, so…"

"Then grab your jacket. I may end up needing someone to keep me from throttling Peahen." She chuckled.

"Do I even want to know?" Agent Hunt asked.

She shook her head. "Probably not, but at the very least we can both get out of the office for an hour and take a ride in America's finest fleet car." She laughed as she motioned toward the window where parked out in front of the building was a late-model Crown Victoria she was sure had likely once belonged to someone sent to a retirement home. In fact, she could have sworn that upon getting in the first time she had smelled baby powder, Bengay and menthol Halls.

"With a line like that, how could a boy say no?" He stood up and grabbed his jacket, holding it over his arm rather than putting it on. The simple action made her wonder if he didn't feel the same drive to constantly be on point, like she did.

Yet, if someone saw him and recognized him as an agent, they would think nothing of his prowess or experience just because he wasn't wearing a jacket. However, if she simply went with her jacket unbuttoned, she would instantly be seen as less authoritative.

She sighed. She had to knock it off. Picking nits would do nothing to stop the infestation of sexism that ran rampant throughout law enforcement. She just needed to buck up, focus on the task at hand and show Agent Peacock who he was dealing with.

Making their way out of the nondescript brick federal building that sat within the heart of the city of Missoula, she stopped and pulled out a stick of gum. She had to kick the sunflower seed habit. That or she would have to step up her running time.

Regardless, as they got into the fleet car, she missed the salty crunch and snap of the sunflower seed shells when she bit down on the kernels. Calories or no, she loved them. Then again, it always seemed like the things she really cared about the most were things that also caused her the most harm.

As she looked in the rearview mirror and put the car in gear, she watched as a black van stopped at the light—directly behind them and blocking their departure.

She didn't like it, the feeling of being trapped in her parking space. It wasn't an emergency by any means, but this lack of foresight when setting this building up for agents like her—people who had places to be—it gnawed at her. If the people in the van wished harm upon her, it would have been easy to follow through. In fact, this was exactly how she would have set it up, by boxing her into her parking spot, then slipping out of the driver's side and silently moving to her window. A quick double tap of the trigger and the driver and the van could pull away within seconds, likely unnoticed and unseen by the general public, and leaving her and Agent Hunt dead.

But maybe she was warped.

No, there was a major difference between paranoid and protective. This, this oversight, was a matter of safety, not her neurosis.

She would need to get a sit-down with the region's special agent in charge, or SAC, and have them look into the logistics.

Moving to grab her phone and send the agent a text, she heard a crunch of metal and the squeal of brakes from behind her. She jerked, looking up. The van behind her was sitting askew, the back end now resting on the hood of a red Miata. A kid was in the car's driver seat. The poor thing looked terrified as he unbuckled his seat belt and stepped out of his car.

Walking to the front of his car, he put his hands over his mouth and squatted down, then stood back up. He mouthed a series of expletives, and from the look on his face, he was likely already envisioning the tongue-lashing he would receive when he told his parents about the accident.

She didn't envy him, or those days.

"Did you see that? Holy crap," Agent Hunt said from beside her.

"I know." She glanced back in the side mirror, watching without being seen.

The side door of the van wheeled open with a characteristic sound of heavy metal grinding against metal. A man, maybe in his early thirties, with dark hair, brooding eyes and a cleft in his chin, stepped out of the van's side door. Just the sight of him made her gut clench. There was something about him, something that drew her in and yet spoke of danger.

She turned in her seat, hoping to get a better view.

As he stepped onto the street, he looked up at her and their eyes met. For a split second, she thought of looking away, but she checked herself. She wasn't a demure woman, no matter how handsome the man whose gaze met hers.

He gave her a stiff nod.

As he turned, he gave her one more appraising glance and rushed to shut the van's door. He moved with the practiced, smooth movements of someone like her—someone who spent their life in the shadows. As the door shut, she looked into the vehicle. Behind him, lining the walls, was a collection of surveillance systems.

Her breath caught in her throat as she instinctively reached for her sidearm.

Not for the first time, her gut was right—the man was nothing but danger.

Chapter Two

He was a broken man. With every day that slipped by, he found himself sinking further and further into his all-consuming sadness. He had to do something to pull out of this funk before he disappeared into himself and his work, forever.

For the last year, ever since Tiff's death, he had been living day to day only through the habitual motion that came with being a private contractor with STEALTH. In truth, they were his saving grace. Though he had worked for a variety of security companies, if it wasn't for the Martins, he wasn't sure he could have gotten on with another contracting group in the state he was in.

He wasn't doing great—even he could admit it. Thinking about it, he wasn't sure he had said more than a word or two in the last month aside from what he had to say for work. Strangely, the realization didn't bother him. He didn't mind being alone.

It was almost a comfort to know he was the silent harbinger of death. He was like a shadow—no, a ghost—who could come and go around the world, doing his job and never really being noticed. He was completely, inarguably free.

Maybe that made him better than most in their line of work. With the ability to be anonymous came the talent to disappear into a crowd. And in being invisible came a great deal of power. The unseen and unnoticed could do anything, go anywhere, take anything and slip away just as unnoticed as they had been when they arrived.

He was a warrior—a Spartan. A man kept at the edges of society to do the things that most were incapable of doing. His only loyalty was to his brothers and sisters in arms and to those they were sworn to protect. He was at worst the monster under the bed, and at best the man who everyone called when there was no one else to save them. But he would never call himself a hero.

Antihero, maybe.

Dealer of death. Maybe.

Instrument of powerful women and men. *Definitely.*

And just as with Tiff, he was merely another piece of a giant puzzle, whose pieces were constantly shifting and swirling until they were destroyed before a real picture appeared. They were part of the action and reaction, the tug-of-war between factions, governments and companies with agendas and guidelines he would never know.

Well, at least usually. This month was far simpler than most. He had been tasked with attempting to hack into a machining company that may or may not have been selling state military secrets to China or another opposing faction. The company had hired them to spy on their employees—and make sure they were not, in fact, selling secrets—and also to check the measures the company had in place to prevent such actions. Millions of dollars, as well as their current and future contracts, were all on the line.

His investigation and attempts to breach through company security measures could literally make or break the business.

No pressure.

As long as the company had done their legwork and vetted, trained and kept their employees and IT personnel reasonably happy, he doubted he would find anything—or at least anybody who was selling secrets. In cases like these, in which there had been a leak or suspected leak of classified information, the breaches were usually not done maliciously or for monetary gain by the person or people responsible. Nine times out of ten, at least in the cases he had surveilled, an employee had merely said something over the phone, in an email or near their at-home smart device. The captured and recorded conversations then fell into the wrong hands, and the person responsible for the breach was none the wiser that they had just lost millions of dollars' worth of secrets. It was seemingly innocuous moments of ineptitude that often led to the biggest corporate losses.

No matter how many classes he taught to these large companies and their employees, their general lack of understanding of how modern infiltration tactics worked appalled him. No matter how many times he tried to tell people that modern tech was a tremendous risk to their secrets, it was amazing how many CEOs, COOs and CFOs still openly talked, emailed and chatted about their company's secrets. More often than not, they didn't spill major secrets in one sitting. Rather, they told the truth and secrets in small, chewable bits—bits that those listening and transcribing could eventually piece together. A ghost could get just about anything so long as they stayed unknown.

Add in a phone call from someone on the infiltration team's staff, and *bingo*—whoever was eliciting information would likely have more than they could even use.

And though he couldn't help but shake his head at the civilian population's general lack of awareness when it came to safety, he couldn't help but be a little grateful. With everyone turning a blind eye to security weaknesses, he had the opportunity to use it to his advantage. The good guys and the bad guys thought the same way. Once a person understood a bit about the human psyche and the common "it can't happen to me" mentality, it was easy to get almost anything he wanted.

He glanced around at the equipment that surrounded him inside the van. This much equipment may have been a bit overkill, but it was better to have it and not need it than need something and not have it—but that could have been the good old Boy Scout in him.

"How much closer you want me to get before you attempt to break into their system through their Wi-Fi?" Mike asked, looking back at him from the driver's seat as they pulled to a stop at the light. "Did Zoey manage to hack in?"

Troy opened his mouth to tell him no, but as he started to speak, he was stopped by the telltale sound of squealing brakes behind them and the inevitable thud and crunch as he was tossed forward from his seat.

Troy landed on his hands and knees between the two front seats in the van. He jumped into action, did a rapid self-assessment and then cleared Mike for injuries. They would both be fine. He glanced back to the equipment. Nothing looked any the worse for wear.

A thin shaft of daylight shone through the base of the van's back doors, and even from where he sat, he could make out the unmistakable red paint of a car's hood wedged under their bumper.

Son of a... Not today. Not right now.

They had a job to do. And the last thing they needed was some local law-enforcement officer poking around. Though he hoped they would be smart enough not to ask too many questions once they established who he and Mike, and STEALTH—the private contracting company that had given him this assignment—were working for.

Federal and international acronyms, those of the law-enforcement kind, with enough weight to them that they could get out of pretty much any situation.

A minor traffic accident was going to be no big deal. Heck, a smile and a nod and it could all be over and they could all be back on their merry ways.

Or at least he hoped so. But, just like in the past, the minute he assumed anything was going to be simple was the minute he got bit squarely in the rear end.

Mike started to unbuckle, going for the door.

"Wait here. I can handle this," Troy said, moving to the back and stepping out of the side door.

"It's just a kid," Mike said, giving him a wary look.

"Don't worry. I'm not going to kill him," Troy said with a chuckle. Who did Mike think he was? He was a man who sought to eliminate the evil from this world, not add to it.

He stepped out of the van, pushing back his hair from his face as the wind caught it. He hated his hair this long, but ever since coming back stateside, he had wanted to shake things up a bit. It wasn't what most people would call lengthy at a few inches, but to him it was past the point of acceptable.

Assessing the area around him, he glanced at the black car with its backup lights on. Looking at him was a woman. Thick brunette hair, the kind he'd like to run his fingers through, hazel eyes and—from what he could see of her—a pinup figure.

He quickly glanced away.

No. She couldn't notice him, or them or this. *I am a ghost. No one sees me.*

He glanced back at the woman, who was now fully turned around and staring at him and the van. He smoothly shut the door and blocked the view of the equipment inside.

As he looked to her, their eyes locked. In that moment, there was no glancing away, no ignoring the ache in his chest and no way he could go unnoticed.

She had *seen* him.

For the first time in a year, someone besides his team had noticed his existence. It was as if in that moment, with those piercing hazel eyes, she made him *real*.

Chapter Three

Once, while at training at Quantico, Kate had walked into a trap she could have never seen coming, and the mistake had consumed her. It was strange and inexplicable, but the man in the rearview mirror made her feel exactly the same way. She had the same sickening knot in her stomach that told her it wasn't just some random coincidence that he had wrecked right into her life.

What if he was watching her?

She tried to shake the feeling off, but couldn't stop herself from devolving into a hyper state of paranoia.

During their live training sessions at Quantico, they were often required to do open surveillance exercises where they too were being surveilled. It was one of her most and least favorite drills. She loved the art that came with the background work and the setup that came before going after their target, but she hated the fear and anxiety that came with constantly looking over her shoulder.

Seeing that van parked behind them in the street—

it made all of her hate and anxiety come crashing back down.

She was never alone.

No matter where she went in the world, or what she did within the Bureau, someone would always be watching over her. And there was always a trap waiting for her if she took one step off the prescribed path.

Before going to work as a special agent, Kate had prided herself on being a rule follower. She was the kind of woman who was perpetually ten minutes early, never came to a party empty-handed and was always on time with her thank-you notes to hosts and hostesses. If she had been raised in the South instead of on the Oregon coast, she would have been the next debutante princess.

It was what had made it an easy choice for her to head directly to the doors of the FBI as soon as she graduated college summa cum laude from Vassar. The physical and psych testing had been no big deal for her to pass, but when it came to spatial awareness and tactical directives, she had struggled. Being able to memorize license plates forward and backward of every car around her, and then keeping track of people's faces, clothes and assumed beliefs and values... It had all been an incredible struggle.

Looking back, she would have happily done three years of organic chemistry over having to go through another round of surveillance training.

She could have never been a spook.

Agent Hunt cleared his throat beside her, pulling her attention back to the moment at hand. "You okay over there?"

She didn't answer. Instead, she glanced back up at the rearview mirror and watched as the dark-haired man walked around to the end of the van and stopped beside the kid. The boy who had rear-ended him was midmeltdown, tears streaking down his adolescent cheeks, and she didn't have to hear his words to know that he was apologizing profusely.

The man from the van reached up and put his hand on the kid's shoulder, but there was something jerky and forced in the way he moved, as if actually touching another person was causing him some kind of physical discomfort.

The strange realization made her smile. At least she wasn't the only one with war wounds.

"Kate?" Agent Hunt asked.

"Huh?"

"I think it would be a good idea if we headed inside. We don't need to get wrapped up in whatever is going on here," Agent Hunt said with a smile. "I should have guessed that things would go all kinds of wheels up the second we try to take a break. The BuGods have it out for us," he said, using the slang for the Bureau.

She chuckled at his lame attempt at a joke. As flat as it fell, she appreciated the fact that when he must have noticed her discomfort, he had gone out of his way to console her in the only way he could. "No matter what anyone says, Hunt, you are a good dude."

Hunt put his hand to his chest and gave her a look of surprise. "What do you mean? Do people really think I'm *not* a good guy? What the hell, man?"

"Last time I checked, I'm not a man. Not with a set of girls like—" She motioned toward her chest.

"Whoa," he said, stopping her midsentence. "I didn't mean *man* to be pejorative."

She laughed, the sound throaty. "Breaking out the big words, you must have known you screwed up right there."

He put his hands up in surrender. "Two rules that can't be broken in our world… No one disrespects you, and—"

"Don't leave your service arm in the bathroom. Plain and simple." She finished his sentence, chuckling.

"One freaking time," Hunt scoffed. "I had the flu. I learned my lesson. One you will never let me forget."

She was playing with him, but she could still make out the unmistakable edge of butt-hurt in his tone. "If you would have done that back at the farm, you would have been out on your ass. You and I both know that you are lucky that I was the one to come across it. If it would have been Agent Raft, you would have been looking for another job—sans gun—within the Bu."

"Blah, blah…" he said, waving her off. "I know. I

owe you one." He reached down and took hold of the door handle, moving to get out of the car. "On that note, I'm not staying here to take any more of your crap. Man or woman, if I wanted my ass kicked, I would stay home."

"How your girlfriend puts up with you, I will never know," she teased.

He opened the door and stepped out, but not before sticking his head back in so he could get the last word. "That may be a mystery, but why you are still single is as clear as an effing bell." He gave her a wilting smile and slammed the door shut before she could get in the final strike.

Dammit. She had started with a lunge and he'd parried, and his riposte was only fair play. She couldn't let his sharp swordlike words plunge too deep, and yet she could still very much feel their mark.

There was no doubt that she needed to be alone. The last man she had dated had been more than three years ago after they had met on a dating app. It had devolved into sexually explicit text messages that she should have known better than to send, text messages that later had come back to haunt her when her private phone records had been brought into a court case. Her texts had cost her the case, as they called into question her credibility.

She'd never been more hurt or angry in all of her life than she had been in the moment when her then boyfriend had taken the stand and told the world all about her sexual preferences. She couldn't blame him for speaking the truth, he'd been under oath and the defense attorney had been playing sleaze-ball, but she'd never make the mistake of trusting another human being for as long as she lived—not even Hunt was free from her stalemate.

After a stern talking-to and a reprimand that had cost her a raise and a move up in the ranks, she had found herself working in the FBI's Missoula field office. In all reality, it was a far better result than she had expected at the time. Luckily, her superior officer had taken pity on her and understood that life and love had a way of cutting the best out at the knees.

After what was the most embarrassing moment of her life, she had vowed never to love again.

Love meant weakness. Weakness meant pain. Pain meant failure. And she couldn't fail, dammit.

There was a popping sound outside her car. The sound was distinct, although it was muffled by her windows. There was only one thing that could make that noise—a rifle.

She turned around in her seat only to see the boy who had been standing behind the van drop to the ground. Had he been hit?

Instinctively, she reached to her sidearm, unholstering it as she hurried out of her car. She moved behind her door as she tried to distinguish which direction the gunfire had come from. The dark-haired man dropped down, covering the boy with his own body as two more rounds tore through the air. There was a ping as the rounds struck the metal siding of the van.

What in the hell was going on? Who was shooting? Who were they shooting at?

She looked toward the west, in the direction of the source of the sound. From where she was located, she spotted the shimmer of a distant scope and a black rifle muzzle just inside a window at the top floor of the apartment building two blocks from them. There was a muzzle flash, but she barely heard the rip of the bullet as it tore through the air and struck the front of the van.

Kate tucked in behind the body of her car, out of the line of sight from what she assumed was the shooter.

"Stay down!" the man atop the boy yelled at her.

Like she needed a reminder that she didn't want some person taking potshots at her.

Then again, if the man lying in the middle of the road thought that she needed his help, he mustn't have had a clue who she was.

He wasn't her enemy.

And yet that didn't guarantee he played for the same side, the side of honor.

Good Samaritan or not, he was involved in something that was causing gunfire to rain down upon them. In her entire career, she'd been in only three active shooter scenarios. None of the shooters in those cases had made it out alive.

She grabbed her handset and radioed in to the

local dispatcher. She identified herself, then continued. "We have an active shooter, possible mass shooting in progress on the 200 block of Pine. Shooter is in the Sol building 400 block of Pine, fifth floor. Requesting all available resources."

The dispatcher cleared her request. There was the crackle and fade in the background as the dispatcher went to work sending the information about the shooting out to all the applicable channels.

She would have all the help she needed in less than a few minutes, but a lot could happen while she waited.

Five rounds pinged through the air and struck the van. She braced for potential impact. Moving so she remained under cover, she glanced at the van's windshield. It had the unmistakable spiderwebbed marks where the shooter's rounds had struck just where a driver's head would have been, but none of them had pierced through. Bulletproof glass. An armored van.

There was a sinking feeling in her gut that told her she was dealing with what people in her line of work called the "icemen." She couldn't be one hundred percent sure, but with a military-grade van, intel equipment and two ghosts…it seemed highly likely that she had just come in contact with corporate espionage.

But what in the hell would intellectual spies be doing in the middle of Montana, where on the most exciting days a bear wandered into the center of the city?

What did I walk into?

There was the piercing wail of police sirens.

If they were smart, whoever was behind the attack was going to be long gone before they arrived.

The window in which she had first spotted the shooter now stood empty, as if only moments before there hadn't been a sniper posted inside, bearing down on her.

She sank to her haunches, taking a moment to collect herself. Her hands were shaking and the realization both surprised and disappointed her.

There had been far more terrifying moments at Quantico, live firing drills and mental warfare, and she'd never reacted like this. Why here? Why now?

Had living in this relatively peaceful city—until this very moment, that was—made her lose her edge?

No one could see her like this.

She bit the inside of her cheek, hard. The taste of coppery blood filled her mouth and pulled her back to reality. This was nothing more than another day in the office. This was nothing to get upset over. Emotions were killers.

Focus.

The man she had first seen get out of the van moved off the boy, who appeared to be okay, just shaken. She guessed he'd dropped at the first sound of the gun or been so startled he'd lost his balance. The man raised his SIG Sauer, and pointing in the direction of the shooter, he helped the boy to safety behind the van, then made his way over toward her.

"Are you okay?" he asked.

She slipped her service arm back into the holster, though as she did, she wasn't exactly sure whether to do so was in her best interest or not. The shooter could come at them from another direction at any moment. And yet the foreboding that had been filling her had subsided.

Though she didn't believe in intuition when it came to her job, there were times when she still adhered to the magic of the feeling.

The dark-haired man extended his hand, an unspoken offer to help her to her feet. She'd always loved a chivalrous man; true gentlemen might have been one of her greatest weaknesses.

Slipping her hand into his, she let him help her up. "I don't see any blood," he said, giving her an appraising, thoughtful glance.

Though she shouldn't have been, she was slightly disappointed in his seeming lack of interest in her ample assets.

She'd always been proud of her décolletage, and yet he was a man who didn't seem to really care.

This iceman was even more cold than the work she presumed he did.

A gentleman who was mysterious, chivalrous and seemingly indifferent to her charms.

Crap.

This kind of wispy, dry ice always had a way of seeping through her armor and straight into her heart. When something that cold met her heart, it would end up only shattered into a million pieces.

Her hand was warm and she realized that she was still holding his as she leaned back against her car. She pulled away.

For the first time in her life, she wished for a firefight. Unlike the man who helped her, snipers presented less danger.

Chapter Four

"I'm Troy," he said, looking at the beautiful woman who had the look of a frightened deer in her eyes.

As soon as his name flew past his lips, the look of fear left her face. "Troy," she said, clipped. "Are you active?"

He tried to control his autonomic response at her overly prying question. He grunted unintelligibly in response, giving her nothing.

Who in the hell was this woman? Using his peripheral vision, in hopes of not giving himself and his inspection away, he looked her over. She was brunette and wearing the dark suit of a professional, but pinned to her lapel was an American flag, and a lanyard was tucked under her shirt, her name badge and tin star hidden from view, but not hidden from those like him who were accustomed to looking for such things.

The FBI really needed to work on their disguises. Or perhaps some of their power lay in the fact that they hid just under the average person's radar. Thanks to his outlier status, and the knowledge that came with it, this lifted veil spoke of her underlying authority. Maybe that was exactly what the Bureau wanted.

He'd always had a sense of antagonism when it came to the BuCrew and their seeming ambivalence to those they deemed "less than," especially since, in the few times he'd worked with their teams, he had found himself labeled as one within that camp.

She gave him a disarming smile, the practiced smile of someone in control.

His hackles rose slightly, but perhaps it was just residual emotions from the firefight. At least he hoped so; he'd never been the kind of man who had been put off by a woman in control—in fact, he always found it a bit of a turn-on. His girlfriend before Tiff had been a CEO for a small manufacturing firm in San Francisco, and was nothing but power…except in the bedroom. There, she was all his.

He tried to ignore the way the woman's jacket pulled tight as she crossed her arms over her chest. If he had to guess, she was a little like his ex—the perfect combination between self-confidence and power mixed with sensuality and acquiescence. Then again, passion and power could have a beautiful place when it came to bedroom activities as well.

His body stirred to life and he looked away and toward the direction where the shooter had been posted. What jerk thought about tits when Mike was sitting in the van and a teenager was leaning shell-shocked on the vehicle?

Work needed his attention. More accurately, they needed to get the hell out of Dodge before their bosses caught wind of what had happened. Not that they would be the first intel officers to find themselves on the wrong end of a set of handcuffs.

Unlike the Bu woman, he didn't have a readily accessible get-out-of-jail-free card; his took a few more phone calls.

When it came to trouble in the form of violence and women, avoidance was best.

He turned his back to the woman, and she let out a little squeak as he walked to the boy. Mike was with him, double-checking to make sure he was unscathed.

"What? What happened?" the boy stammered, his eyes wide. His pants were wet, a common result of this type of event, and a sense of pity filled Troy.

This was one day that was going to stick with this kid forever. He'd probably wake up sweating in the night. Question his role in the accident and the precursors to the shooting. He would blame himself.

Troy would have to make an effort to check on the kid's welfare for the next few years. An event like this often had two unexpected consequences for a kid: moving forward and using the violence to his benefit, or tarnishing his trust in humanity and imbuing the boy with a sense of fear so great that it would lead to further violence or death. He had to hope that, for the kid's sake, he would find himself coming down with a savior complex.

"It's going to be okay…" He paused, hoping the kid would give him his name.

"John."

Good—he was off to a good start in getting the boy calmed down.

There were footsteps behind him as the FBI woman came over. "John, it's great to meet you. I'm Kate Scot. I'm an agent with the Federal Bureau of Investigation. I'm here to let you know that everything is going to be okay."

She was about as subtle as a fist to the face. And people judged him for his line of work. He sighed, and she sent him a sideways glance.

A police cruiser pulled up and onto the corner, three more in its wake, effectively closing down the intersection and boxing them in, trapping him. He resisted the urge to retreat into the shadows and disappear before there was no longer an option and he was incapacitated; these were the good guys. They were doing their jobs. He didn't have to like it, just accept their actions for what they were—an attempt to keep the general public safe.

Besides, they were good, but he was better. If he wanted out, he'd get out.

No cage was strong enough to keep him.

A string of LEOs rolled out of the car as the men and women flooded out from inside the federal building.

"The shooter disappeared. We need to cordon off

an area four blocks wide. Shut everything down," Agent Scot ordered, taking control of the scene as she motioned for the crews to move out.

There was a flurry of motion as the city police officers went into action.

They could do as much as they wanted, but given the limited resources and the size of the city, the chances of getting their hands on the shooter were slim to none. At least, not right away. First, they needed to get their hands on witnesses, anyone who could have possibly seen the shooter coming or going from the building.

The one thing they did have going for them was that Missoula was a city small enough for people to take note of each other. It wasn't like New York, where the population was just a faceless audience in an individual's life.

The man who had initially been in the car with Agent Scot rushed over to her side. "You okay?" the man asked, giving her an evaluating glance, one that made an odd and unwelcome wiggle of possessiveness move through him.

What in the hell was wrong with him?

There was a tap on his shoulder. Mike was standing behind him. "We need to get out of here. There are too many people sniffing around. If we don't get out now, our entire mission is going to be compromised. You know Zoey will have our asses if we aren't careful."

Zoey Martin, their boss at STEALTH, would have

their asses regardless of what they did. That woman was hell on wheels, and yet they loved her all the more for her unflappability and take-no-crap attitude.

Mike slipped back into the van and Troy moved to follow. As he opened the door of their van, a hand gripped his wrist from behind. Instinctually, he raised his elbow, readying himself to strike whoever dared to touch him.

"Where do you think you're going?" Agent Scot asked.

He lowered his elbow, gently twisting his wrist to break her grasp, but she held on only tighter. Yielding, he stopped. "I have a job to do."

"You can't leave the scene without someone taking a statement. And what about the kid?" she asked, pointing in the direction of the boy who had started this fiasco.

"Let him go. We will take care of our end of things, accident-wise. He is going to have one hell of a crappy day without adding our repair bill to his list of concerns. Call it a Christmas gift."

She chuckled, but the sound was dark and matched the world around them. "First, Christmas is six months away. Second, you can't think that we are going to let you take this van. It is critical evidence in our investigation. You better get real comfortable while we unscrew this situation."

"I have a job to do. *We* have a job to do," he said,

motioning toward Mike, who was sitting back in the driver's seat.

"I don't care if you are the president and are on your way to the Oval Office. Your van and both of you are staying here. The only question is whether it will be thanks to handcuffs or not."

Dammit.

That jumped to handcuffs a hell of a lot faster than he had anticipated. It was too bad that her first reference to handcuffs involved a crime scene instead of a bedroom activity.

"And don't think I don't know exactly who in the hell you are and what you do," she said, her voice barely above a whisper.

His blood ran cold. If she knew who he was, he was as good as dead. Had his identity been compromised? Was that how the shooter had found them?

If people knew him, there would be other killers to follow. He had an enemies list at least as long as his arm, and not half as dignified.

She had to have been playing him. Damn, he hoped so.

"Then who am I?" he asked, hoping she would falter.

"Do you want to play that game, Iceman?"

He tensed, trying to hide the response by slipping out of her grip once and for all. He didn't need her taking his pulse and acting like a human lie detector. Some things he could control, but his heart wasn't one of them.

"I have no idea what you are talking about." His rebuttal sounded feeble and understated even to his own ears.

"You can try to lie to me all you want, but John Q doesn't roll around a small Montana town with a half-a-million-dollar van filled with spy equipment." She paused. "Who do you work for?"

Oh, hell no.

He opened his mouth, but she put her hand up and stopped him midvowel.

"And don't you start the nonsense about 'If I told you, I'd have to kill you.' We both know that is crap, and neither of us has time for that kind of stupidity. So, in an effort for transparency and if we are possibly going to be joining forces, you need to tell me the truth."

His appreciation for her compounded tenfold. In other circumstances, he would have happily worked to get this woman into his bed—handcuffs or no.

Stop.

Though he liked to think of himself as a man who respected women and their boundaries, rare moments like these made him wonder if he needed to work on his self-awareness. Beautiful, filled with spunk and courage, she attracted him. It was really too bad that she wasn't more of a terror. Then at least he could tell himself that she wasn't his type, but as it stood, she was entirely too much like a woman he could have been interested in.

"Answer me, and quit playing games," she pressed.

He had to check his grin. Though he hadn't been trying to keep her on her toes, it appeared he was doing exactly that. And she was reading it as him trying to control the conversation.

She must have been thinking him far smarter than he thought himself.

"If I tell you who I am, I need you to make me a promise."

She raised her brow, giving him a doubtful look. "What?"

His gut roiled. Everything in his life depended on his abilities to stay in the shadows and remain unseen. Though he would never call himself anything remotely close to a hero, he did strive to work for the greater good and be the person who saved lives of people he would never meet and who would never know the sacrifices he made for their safety. If he was outed, his life and the lives of the people whom he strove to help would all be put into danger. And that was to say nothing about his job. Even if he managed to live through the exposure, he would have nothing left—arguably, he would be better off dead.

The Russian proverb came to mind: *Doveryáy, no proveryáy.* Trust, but verify.

Unfortunately, in a situation like this, verification would have to come quickly.

"Do you play politics?" he asked.

She frowned. "That's not a promise."

"Just answer me."

"I avoid them like the plague," she said, looking over her shoulder.

That would have to do, for now. "If I tell you who I am, and who I work for, I need to trust that you can keep it a secret. I need your protection."

Her mouth opened and closed twice before she seemed to find the words she was struggling to say. "You can trust me."

"My life depends on it." He reinforced his words by reaching down and touching her hand. "Truly."

"I'm yours...your ally." She looked him in the eye. There were dark brown flecks interspersed throughout her hazel eyes.

Though there was no one standing too close, and even those who were close enough to hear were far too busy to be listening, he leaned into her. She smelled like coffee and sunflower oil, but beneath the smell of her office was the jasmine scent of her body wash. "I'm an operator with STEALTH."

She took a big step back from him, but he wasn't sure if it was because of his candor or his proximity.

"You work for the Martins?" she asked, her voice airy and any disbelief she may have had now completely gone.

He nodded.

She ran her hands down over her face, smearing her black eyeliner at the corner of her left eye. He wanted to reach up and clear the smudge for her, but he already felt vulnerable and he didn't need to make things worse.

Agent Scot swallowed hard. "With you here, it's no wonder there was a shoot-out. It's a miracle that anyone was left standing."

Chapter Five

There was trust, and then there was "I am trusting you with my life" trust. Few and far between had ever asked such a thing of her, and rarely in the first five minutes of knowing their name.

Wait—he'd never even told Kate his full name.

She thought about asking him his personal details—she would need them for her investigation—but at the same time, if she pressed him, she wasn't sure he would give her a real answer. She had worked with his kind before, and his kind weren't known for giving their trust even when they were on the same team. Trust was something that had to be earned and then tried before the recipient even knew it was a viable option.

This man was good in all the wrong ways; he was going to be nothing but a pain in her ass. Yet she didn't shirk from the possibility of being nearer to him.

Though there was no doubt that she shouldn't have been drawn to bad boys, there was something primitive in her need to be with them. Thankfully, she'd learned to quell that pull ever since her college boyfriend—Alex, a marine who'd loved to tell her that she needed to lose twenty pounds while he stuffed his face with Cheetos. She could have still punched him in the face. But she'd heard it said that a person had to really love to really hate.

Her cell phone buzzed from inside her pocket and she pulled it out. Fifteen missed calls and twice that in texts. Even the crew in Salt Lake City had tried to contact her. Word had spread fast about the shooting.

"I want you to know, I had nothing to do with what happened here today," the dark-haired man said. "But whoever pulled that trigger…they had to have known that I was coming. Which means that if I don't get the hell out of here, I'm putting myself and my team at risk. If you need me, you know how to get in touch." He bladed his feet, moving toward the sidewalk.

"You're not going anywhere," she said, sounding more authoritarian than she felt next to the man. "I appreciate what you are saying, but I can't let you go. No matter who you work for. Zoey and I are friends. I can give her a call and get you cleared by your team if you'd like, but I need you. As I see it, you are the reason this all went down, even if you don't think you are. They weren't shooting at me, and they weren't shooting aimlessly at the people on the street. Whoever was behind this, they were going for a kill shot on your driver. They just underestimated their opponents."

His jaw clenched as he seemed to be trying to cover his tells and his body language. The attempt told her more than if he had spoken—he knew she was right. At least he was smart enough not to try to deny her rationale.

"Iceman, how good are you at your job?" she asked.

"Until this morning?"

She chuckled. "You want to go with me while I clear the floors?"

It was dangerous bringing this stranger with her and there were better ways to keep him under her team's thumb, but no one would keep better control of him than her.

His eyes widened. "Seriously?"

"How long have you been in the game?" From the little crow's-feet around his eyes and his fading tan, she guessed he was about thirty and had been in the desert not too long ago.

"Contracting?"

"Let's say all special security operations," she said, hoping to lead him.

"I've been at it long enough to know how to clear a building and get my hands on a shooter."

Of course, that would be his answer. "Then don't let me down and don't leave my ass hanging." She waved for him to follow her as she yelled commands out at her team. "Hunt, you head the scene here. We're going to do a sweep at the shooter's location."

"Roger that," Agent Hunt said, a frown on his face.

She charged down the road, clearing as she worked toward the Sol building. There was a SWAT team posted at the building's doors, and as she approached, the sergeant waved at her to stop until she lifted her badge, flashing it for clearance.

"Did you get a visual on our shooter?" she asked.

The sergeant lowered his assault rifle to his side, the action seeming somehow resigned. "Not yet. However, we found evidence that he may have discarded his clothes in a dumpster behind the building."

Crap.

Their shooter was among them, and smart as hell.

"Did you pull any lookie-loos who spotted the shooter? Saw his face?" she asked.

The sergeant pinched his lips and shook his head. "No one so far. You guys will have more luck."

Yeah, the SWAT crew was more concerned with kicking doors than they were with collecting statements.

"We swept the fifth floor. Dude left his gun. MK12 Model 1."

She nodded. This guy must have been planning on leaving the gun behind all along. Either he was superconfident it held no clues to his identity, or he'd planted false ones on it. Or he was just careless.

There were far better, more expensive sniper guns out there. If she was going to pull the trigger like the man had, she would have used the M110 SASS. Something like that would have run between eight to ten thousand, versus the couple-thousand-dollar model that the shooter had dumped.

Then she was assuming that money was some kind of deciding factor. If their sniper was being funded by a paramilitary, corporation or government, a price point for a leftover gun was probably the last thing on their minds.

She couldn't assume anything yet, but the more details she could piece together, the more she could try to build a profile around their shooter, their identity and their motive.

The iceman stepped around her. "Did they leave any brass?"

The sergeant looked him up and down, feeling him out for a fed. "Who in the hell are you?"

He chuckled. "Call me Troy."

"Well, *Troy*, as a matter of fact, there were at least a dozen spent casings. What the hell does that matter?" The sergeant spit out his name, making her wonder if they were having some kind of caveman fight over the woman—her—in their presence.

Men.

"Keep your guys on scene," she said, trying to ignore the battling testosterone around her. "Let me know if you find anything else. And make sure to send me pictures of the area in which you found the clothes. My team will be in shortly to collect the evidence."

"10-4," the sergeant said, turning toward his crew.

They made their way inside and she could sense

that Troy wanted to take the lead in the way he kept pressing in close from behind her. He was so close; she was almost certain that if she held her breath she could have heard his heart beat.

The building was silent, the kind of quiet that came just after a storm, a quiet that promised that there was more to come, but it was only a matter of time.

SWAT had cleared the building, but the electricity that came with fear and crime still filled the air.

"Take three steps back," she ordered as they reached the bottom of the stairwell. Her voice echoed against the concrete, bouncing until it disappeared into the shadows overhead.

From behind her, she could make out the distinct sound of steel scraping against hard plastic as he pulled his sidearm from its holster. She followed suit, slipping her gun out, though she doubted she would have to pull the trigger. It was better to be safe than wish she had been at the ready.

She moved forward, Troy giving her space. Their footfalls filled the quiet air, the only other sound their breathing as they ascended the staircase. The fifth floor was deadly silent, as if even the building knew what had happened within its core.

It was all office spaces, most completely abandoned and neglected, with dusty boxes in their corners and the windows covered with old newspapers. The door was open to the office space that had held the shooter. There was an old desk in front of the window. Upon it sat the assault rifle, mounted on a tripod and lifted with sandbags.

On the desk were the spent casings.

She put away her weapon, took out her camera and started snapping pictures from a variety of angles, hoping to catch things that she was yet to notice. She'd have plenty of time back in the office to dissect the images, but for now she had to look at the big picture.

From where she stood, she could see people milling around Troy's van. It wasn't a difficult shot to hit the van; in fact, it was the perfect setup.

"I don't think the boy, John, was in on the shooting."

Troy shook his head as she looked back at him. "Nah, the kid was just at the wrong place at the wrong time."

"You want to tell me what led up to the accident?"

"I told you… I didn't have—"

"Anything to do with the shooting," she said, finishing his sentence. "But we both know that you can't deny you were the target. You said it yourself. But that's not what I was asking. I was asking what led up to the accident." She paused, looking at him.

He was staring at the floor as if, somewhere in the dust, he could find the words that she wanted to hear.

"If you want me to protect you, to keep your secret, then we are going to have to start out with some goddamned truths. Do you understand me?" she pressed.

He looked up at her. "What do you really want to know?"

"Who would want you dead? At least today?"

"It could be any number of people." He sighed. "This shooter, they could have been after me or Mike. It's hard to tell."

"How long have you been working with your driver? He's a contractor too, right?"

"Mike's my brother. I would trust him with my life. And we've been working tight together for the last two years. I'm the one who got him into the game—for better or worse." A certain guilt seemed to tinge his words.

"What's your last name? Are you one of the Martins?"

"No. My name is Troy, Troy Spade."

She gave him the side-eye as she tried to watch him for any deceptive behaviors.

"I'm telling the truth. And, to be honest, it's the first time I've spoken my full, real name since I was hired on at STEALTH."

"Are you operating under an alias?"

He simply nodded. "It's possible that the company I'm investigating is the one behind this," he said, motioning around the room.

"What company is that?" she asked.

"They are called ConFlux. They have a headquarters downtown and—"

"Are associated with military machining," she

said, interrupting and finishing his sentence as all the blood drained from her face.

"You know them?"

She nodded, the motion slow and smooth. "Yeah, I'm familiar."

Troy said nothing, just watched her as if he could hear there was more to the story and was simply going to outwait her for the details.

There was no use in holding out.

"ConFlux is owned by my family. My father is the CEO. My mother… She used to run the financials, but retired five years ago."

A quick curse escaped his mouth. Then he remained mute, his entire body tense and his pupils dilated as his fight response appeared to kick in. Nothing could have prepared her for this, for staring down her enemy…an enemy who had just entrusted her with his life.

She thought she had known true silence, but as she stood in that room with the man who had been sent to investigate her family's company, the world around her became deafeningly quiet.

Chapter Six

That was what he got for believing in trust, even if it was only for a millisecond. What the hell had he been thinking in giving the woman his real name without more vetting? Dammit.

Know thine enemy.

Lesson number one. He had known the owner had a daughter and she was local, but in all of his background work, he'd found nothing to indicate that she was working for the FBI. The only thing he had found about the girl, Kate, was some high school track stats and a picture from when she was out with her friends—she'd been around sixteen. The gangly, awkward girl he had seen looked nothing like the stunningly beautiful, confident agent who now stood beside him.

This kind of thing, this right here, was going to get him killed. And screw it, if it was his fault and he died it was one thing…but if Mike got hurt or killed because of the mistake, he was never going to forgive himself.

He had to go into damage control before something happened that he couldn't take back.

"If it makes you feel better, I don't think that your 'rents have anything to do with this shooting. At least, I hope not," he lied through his teeth, trying to cover the tells he knew she was searching him for. "Besides, what would your parents have to hide or cover up?" He could hear himself blabbering; he needed to shut the hell up, so he pinched the inside of his arm with his hand as he moved to holster his weapon.

Though he wasn't sure he had sold his lies well enough, especially with the verbal diarrhea that had escaped his lips, she let out a relieved sigh.

"My parents are good people. They haven't had any kind of trouble—at least, none I know of—since they started the company. You're right. They wouldn't do something like this."

He walked around the room, careful not to disturb the scene. The SWAT team had been right about the weapon, but of course they would be knowledgeable about such things—it was their job. He bent down, looking closer at one of the spent casings, not touching the brass.

Often, the one way shooters made a mistake was when they failed to cover their tracks while loading their weapon. He'd heard of more than a few cases being solved thanks to rogue fingerprints on brass or a hair caught in the magazine. It was the little things that always screwed a person.

"See something?" she asked, moving beside him and looking over his shoulder.

It was good that she wasn't a little thing. She had more power in her stature and presence than most, and damn if it didn't make him ache for her to step just a little bit closer.

He turned to face her, careful to avoid the tension that threatened to erupt between them. With the naked eye, he couldn't see a print, but he wasn't about to mess with possible trace evidence by handling the round. Instead, he moved closer and to the right for a better look. From the outside, it appeared typical and one of a million others like it, and yet there was more to it than most would realize. "This is the NATO 5.56 casing."

She stared at him like he had grown a horn out of the middle of his forehead. "What are you thinking?"

"Just that whoever pulled the trigger knew their craft. This round is consumed en masse by military and police officers alike. As for the general public, it's a known quantity but harder to get."

"You think that our shooter was military or law enforcement?"

He shrugged. "It's a place to start. Though, most of the military guys I work with usually use Federal brand rounds. It's more of a personal preference thing, but whatever..." He slowly stood up, feeling like a complete dork for going down the rabbit hole that was munitions and guns. "Did you get enough pictures?" He motioned toward her phone.

"I think I have gotten everything here." She slipped her camera back into her pocket as she walked toward the window and looked outside.

Her body was silhouetted by the midday light, and he couldn't help but notice the faint line where her panty pulled against her hip beneath her suit trousers. Damn, he would have loved to run his finger right over that spot, to touch her skin, to feel her silky underwear in his hands.

Whoa—where had that come from? He was a professional, on a job, and though he appreciated a good-looking woman as much as the next man, he'd locked down those kinds of strong feelings for a while. *Don't touch, don't be touched, don't get hurt.* That was his new mantra.

Looking away, he walked toward the office's door.

The place had the distinct odor of spent gun powder and sweat. "Whoever our shooter was, they must have been sitting up here for hours waiting for their shot."

"Why do you say that?"

"Take a deep breath," he said. "Smell that? This dude was ripe."

She squinted her eyes, like she was trying to decide whether or not he was messing with her, but then she cracked a smile. "I thought a rat had died in the wall or something. You telling me that's man?"

"Clearly, you haven't spent enough time in a Connex with twenty other dudes," he said with a laugh. "This is nothing. After a while in a container unit, you start considering how many rounds you would be willing to take just so you don't have to lie next to a bunch of dudes after egg MREs."

She laughed out loud. "You did not just go there."

He had to admit that he loved the sound of her laugh. It was clean and bright, coming from a place deep within her that he doubted rarely saw the light of day. He'd give a lot to hear that sound again. "You went with the dead rat. You started this," he said, laughing.

Damn, he could get used to this.

Truth be told, the only person he'd been talking to as of late was Mike and, like living in the Connex, it made him consider going rogue.

"Let's go," she said, walking past him and out into the hall.

She took a deep breath of the nonfetid air. He'd gotten to her, and the conniving part of him kind of loved it. There was something about this kind of nuanced game that stoked his soul, even if there was no chance of anything more than them becoming friends. With her, he would take what he could get.

He felt a vague flicker deep within, as if some ember was being sparked to life, something he'd not sensed in a long time. It caused both pain and joy. He tried not to think of the pain.

Their footfalls sounded on the concrete as they made their way downstairs. They slipped out of the back of the building, and there was the dumpster that the SWAT team had mentioned. Beside it were two tac'd-up SWAT members. They were holding their ARs to their chests like they were their life-lines. He'd always appreciated a locked and loaded Spec Ops team, but it may have been overkill when it came to guarding the trash.

The team leader bobbed his head, acknowledging Kate, but he did little to cover the contempt in his face when he glanced over at Troy. He didn't blame the guy. If he saw some grunt following around on the heels of a good-looking agent, he would have wondered what the hell was up too.

"Anyone see anything?" she asked.

The guy shook his head.

She took out her camera and took pictures of the dumpster. Opening up the lid a bit wider, he could make out desert khaki tactical pants and a gray hoodie. After getting a variety of pictures, she motioned for the SWAT guy. "Have your team bag these up and drop them off at Evidence. I'll have my team take care of them from there."

"10-4," the man said.

She moved away from the team, her face awash with concentration. He wished he could know what she was thinking. If he was in charge of this investigation, they wouldn't have been standing around; he would have been calling in drones and moving satellites in order to get a pin on their shooter. But then again, this wasn't his investigation and this wasn't a war-torn region of some developing nation. This was America, home of the brave and the situationally unaware.

He regularly forgot how different his view was of the world—that was, until he was back down in the reality of living in a nation where safety had given rise to comfort and comfort had given rise to blindness.

Not that Kate was blind.

He walked behind her like a lost puppy, heading back to the car crash scene, feeling more and more out of place every second he was forced to follow. "If you wanted, I could—" He started to speak, but she stopped him with a touch.

"You don't get to go anywhere." She looked annoyed as she lifted her cell phone to her ear and started speaking to someone on the other end.

"Yeah, anything?" she said.

He wasn't trying to eavesdrop, but she wasn't trying to disguise her conversation, either.

Kate watched him as the person on the other end of the line must have been speaking.

"See what you can pull. No crosshatching on the brass. Normal markings." She continued giving a report of what they had seen. After a few minutes, she clicked off the call and moved to send whomever she had been talking to the pictures she had taken.

He was dying to ask her the specifics of her conversation, but as much as he was curious, he wouldn't—if someone asked him questions like that, the last thing they would get would be any real answers.

"So, tell me more about you," she said, turning back to him. She motioned for him to follow her in the direction from which they had come. "What brings you here, besides my family's company?"

He was really hoping she had forgotten about that admission. Fat chance. She was too smart to let it go, and it was just this kind of thinking that drew him toward her.

"Who were you talking to?" he asked, trying to turn the conversation away from anything that would cause him discomfort or lead him into making any more mistakes.

"That was Agent Hunt. No one has spotted our shooter, so it looks like we are going to be working from the ground up. However, we do have beat cops working the perimeter. They put up roadblocks. Yet I have a feeling that, given the professionalism of our shooter, we have a better chance of finding Waldo."

He glanced around the area. Unlike many metropolitan cities, Missoula was conspicuously devoid of any eyes in the sky. Until now, it was one of the reasons he had enjoyed doing the job he did in this state. He didn't need to worry about his actions being tracked. The lack of tech was probably a major thorn in her side, though, especially if she had ever worked in the tech sectors within the Bureau.

Once again, he was reminded of how little he could gather about her. He'd like to know a lot more, not just for anything related to his job but because she intrigued him. For now, all he could glean from her would have to come from watching and listening, looking for patterns and tells in her person.

Right now, she was standing tall, confident in her abilities and who she was as a person. Maybe she felt that way, maybe she was putting on a show just for him. The truth would come out, eventually.

"If I were you, and I'm not saying you don't know how to do your job, but I would start having my guys tap into all the camera systems within three miles. There are a limited number of choke points in this city. If you look close enough at who is coming and going, I'm sure we can get a visual on this guy."

Her brows rose. "I have my crew working on that, among a few other things."

Raising his hands, palms up, he showed his surrender. "I didn't mean anything—was just trying to give you some helpful suggestions, maybe a starting block or two."

"A good starting block would be to get a key on why someone would want to shoot you and Mike down there," she said, motioning in the direction of his van.

Mike was handcuffed, his hands tight between his back, and he was leaning against the federal building. The man beside him, who Troy recognized as Agent Hunt, was talking on the phone. He was waving his hands around, and the way his face puckered made Troy wonder if the guy was talking to one of the STEALTH crew.

Troy chuckled under his breath. Mike's face was pinched into a tight scowl, and even from a block away, he could read his lips loud and clear. He was an unhappy camper, and he could only guess what Mike had said that had led to him getting a set of silver bracelets. If a bad guy had tried restraining his brother, they would have ended up in a body bag.

"If you want me to tell you anything, we're going to have to be on the same team." He pointed at his brother. "If you don't have your guys let him go, there is no way on this green earth that I'm going to talk to you…with or without handcuffs."

Kate looked over at his brother and then motioned to the agent beside him. "What in the hell are you thinking?" she yelled, jogging slightly to get over to them and through the crowd of officers and bystanders that had started to accumulate in the wake of the shooting. "Folks, this is an active crime scene!"

The people milling around barely seemed to notice the woman yelling in their midst.

There was an older man milling about, talking to someone on his telephone. His eyes were wide and his words were coming fast as he paced, all evidence of stress behavior.

As he watched the man, he was reminded how different he was from the public; he didn't have the same response. He'd gone through far too many rapid stress adaptation drills for something like a little shooting to get under his skin. Everyone was alive and unhurt. What more could people want?

He followed behind Kate as she made her way to Mike. His brother's face was tight and red, and he could only imagine how the conversation would go once they got the hell away from this S-show.

Though it seemed impossible, Mike was a guy who liked sticking deeper to the shadows than him. Mike was a night owl, wanting to do nothing more than watch, listen and document his enemies. When he did pull the trigger, he only had to pull it once. But it had been a long time since Mike had been the one to draw down. Though, right in this moment, Troy held no doubts that it was exactly what Mike wanted to do.

His brother was maturing as a person; if nothing else, he would have to buy him a beer later and congratulate him on his personal growth.

Mike looked over at him, and as he spotted Kate, he stopped talking and stood up a bit against the building, puffing his chest out.

Maybe he had a little bit more personal growth to go—especially when it came to the fairer, and arguably wiser, sex.

Agent Hunt said something and Mike turned around as the officer reached for the cuffs, but he didn't take his eyes off Kate. An odd wave of possessiveness washed over Troy and he took an almost imperceptible movement closer to the woman. Mike must have seen it because he sent him a sly grin as he approached.

Slipping the cuffs off, Mike turned back around and rubbed his wrists. He glared at Agent Hunt. "I would like to reiterate that putting me in cuffs was more than a little unprofessional, ass—"

"Nope, don't say it," Troy said, cutting his brother off before he spouted something that they would both come to regret. "Kate, this is Mike Spade. He is a fellow contractor…" He sighed. "And this piece of meat is my brother, for better or worse."

She extended her hand, but not without Troy noticing that Mike was staring at her chest region. "Nice to meet you, Mike. You are a fellow contractor?"

Mike gave him a WTF look that made him yearn to flip his brother the bird. *He* wasn't the one who'd had to be rescued from cuffs; Mike had no business to judge.

"It's okay—your brother and I have established that we are on a trajectory that is going to need some fine-tuning and honesty. If not, your next trajectory will be to jail—no matter how much I like Zoey and the rest of the Martins."

Mike's eyebrows shot up with surprise. "You know the Martins?"

She laughed. "This is far too small of a town for us *not* to know your bosses. We've had a few run-ins with their *friends* in the past."

"If you like Zoey, then you are off to a good start with me." Some of the tension eased from Mike's body. "But I can't say the same about my brother… or his big goddamned mouth."

"Your brother is tighter than a snare drum, so

don't jump down his throat too much," Kate said, surprising him.

Why had she risen to his defense?

He glanced over at her, and for a split second, their eyes met. Those hazel eyes… They would be the end of him. Even if they were hedging their bets with one another, he couldn't deny that she was one of the most beautiful women he had ever met. Her long brunette hair had started to gather at the back of her neck where it rubbed against her suit jacket.

Tiff had always hated to wear her hair down. She complained that it got into a rat's nest in the back. For a while Tiffany had tried to wear it loose anytime they weren't training or on assignments, but after six months she had decided that when it came to pleasing him, keeping her tresses free and flowing wasn't worth the effort. He had totally understood. Not long after, she had cut six inches off her hair. She'd never been more beautiful. And then a month later…she was gone.

Yes, he couldn't get involved with another woman— not even the beautiful Kate Scot, despite the instant connection he'd felt with her, the light that had flicked back on deep inside. Sure, they had a lifestyle in common, maybe even a way of thinking and a schedule that was like his own, but they were far too alike for a real relationship. But she had made an effort to keep him happy in her investigation. That had to count for something. Yet he couldn't make the mistake of falling for anyone. When he did, it ended only in heartbreak and death—Tiffany was proof of that.

If he hadn't gotten involved with her, she would have probably worked with a different unit, she wouldn't have gotten into the up-armored vehicle with him, and there were a million other little things that she had done to put herself in the line of fire for him. Love had made them both blind, and worse—blind to the dangerous world that they had chosen.

No matter what he yearned for, he wouldn't put another person he cared about at risk.

Chapter Seven

There were mistakes, and then there were getting-people-killed mistakes. And she had the sinking feeling that Troy Spade was about to become one of those mistakes.

He sat in the interrogation room inside the federal building; he'd been there for the last two hours. Against Agent Hunt's wishes, she had ordered everyone sandwiches and drinks from Doc's and had them delivered while the rest of her teams cleaned up the streets and sent her emails with all the superfluous details she would have to spend the rest of the night poring over.

She glanced up at the video feed and watched as Mike and Troy sat at the interrogation table, finishing up their lunches. Mike was talking animatedly, but she couldn't make out exactly what he was telling his brother.

Though Troy had told her that they were brothers, looking at them on the feed, it was hard to see their likeness. Troy was taller and his hair was darker than that of Mike's, who was shorter and a tad on the heavier side. They both had the V-shaped, muscular torso that came with a military contractor lifestyle, a life that was made or broken on a person's ability to get themselves out of any catastrophic event in which they found themselves—even when they were an iceman.

She had met a few contractors in her years at the Bureau, and a few of her friends had even left the agency in order to go into the private security sector. The money was always one heck of a draw. The feds paid her just enough to keep her, but not a heck of a lot more.

Contractors raked it in. But, for what it was worth, the men she had run into that lived in that world never saved up… Instead, they had made it to burn it and had an attitude of "We're all gonna die soon, so spend it all now."

It wasn't one of her favorite qualities.

It made her wonder what kind of man Troy was, if he was one of the typical contractors who didn't give a single thought to tomorrow as today was still up for grabs.

She walked to the interrogation room and tapped on the door. Mike's deep baritone voice silenced. "You guys done making up in there, or do you want another minute or two?"

"Just giving each other back rubs in here—you are good," Troy said. "But if Mike doesn't watch himself, he's going to get another chewing."

Kate laughed as she walked in and came over to the table. The interrogation room was soft and friendly, designed to put people at ease. There was a couch against the wall; in front of it was a table covered in a variety of magazines, including everything from *Guns & Ammo* to *Tactical Life*. Maybe she needed to talk to someone about getting a little *Cosmo* up in this joint. Not everyone wanted to read about grain weights and the benefits of a new butt plate.

"I hope you don't mind having to wait in here," she started.

"And I hope you know that it is about the last goddamned place we want to be," Mike said, his voice barely more than a growl. "There you were, touting that we should be allies, and you stick us up in this closet."

"But I did feed you," she said, straddling a chair as she sat down across from them. She picked at a piece of a leftover sandwich and popped a bit of the bread into her mouth like it could act as some kind of salve to the animosity that Mike felt toward her. "And if you wanted, we could head out and get a couple beers once my investigation is complete. I'd love to pick your brains a little bit more about what you do and how a girl like me could get into it." She sucked in a breath, just deep enough to make her breasts press against her shirt.

Yeah, she totally wasn't above using her body

as a weapon. Especially when it came to two door kickers.

Mike stopped talking while Troy gave her a knowing and deflating smile.

"How did you guys become cybersecurity experts?"

Troy put his hands up, palms facing her. "Look, we aren't what I would call 'cybersecurity experts.' Rather, we are both guys who are just doing what we get paid to do… And it may or may not involve a little bit in the tech world."

"I've heard a hell of a lot of hedging and dismissing titles in my day, but you and I both know that what you just said has to be one of the biggest loads of garbage anyone has ever tried to hand my way," she said, throwing Troy a cut-the-crap look.

He chuckled. "All I meant is that there are players in the CS world who are a hell of a lot better than we are, more experienced and a heck of a lot better at writing code."

"And yet you are paid… and paid well, I would assume…in the private securities world," she argued. "I'm not a stupid woman, and I would appreciate it if you would treat me with just a small amount of respect. Let's start by dropping the bull with each other. I didn't get to where I am in the FBI without being good at something. You didn't get where you are without being good at what you do."

Mike laughed as he looked toward his brother.

"Hey, man, you finally found your match. Good luck with this."

Troy smirked at him, and the simple back-and-forth between the two made her like them both just a little bit more. It would have been fun to be a member of their tribe, running operations with them—even if it was in the back of their van.

He glanced over at her. "I'm not being dismissive of our abilities, just honest. We are good, but there are better. We are more specialized than the normal contractors. Mike and I both started out playing in the Sandbox in the fertile crescent area. From there, it was a bunch of hits and misses."

He was hardly the first of his kind who had started his career in the Middle East, nor would he be the last. Many men who came out of a variety of government agencies came home, retired and didn't know what their next steps should be. Some became lobbyists, took positions in governmental offices, and others just couldn't get enough of the fray and went back to work in the private sectors. Mike and Troy were definitely of the latter group.

They were kick-ass-and-take-names types, all in the shadow world of counterintelligence. And she'd be lying if it didn't make Troy look about ten degrees hotter than she already saw him. Dammit, she needed to ignore her weakness for the mysterious hero types.

There was a picture of the St. Andrews Golf Course on the wall above Troy's head, and she forced herself to look at it for a long moment. Anything to not look at him, but make it appear as if she was. He was in the hot seat, but if she wasn't careful in ignoring his odd but magnetic charms, she would find herself there instead. No, thanks.

There was a knock on the door and it cracked open. Her father stuck his head in the entry. "Kate, can I talk to you for a second?"

She couldn't have been more surprised if the Easter Bunny had hopped into the room carrying a basket of grenades.

"Dad?" As soon as she spoke, she realized her misstep in recognizing him in front of the two men she had been trying to dig into. She turned to them. "Excuse me for a moment," she said, standing up.

"Actually, this affects them," her father said, motioning toward the two men. "I'm here to let you know that this questioning needs to come to an end. You are done here."

Though a million comebacks flipped into the front of her mind, she said nothing and instead took her father by the hand and led him out of the room. "What are you doing here, Dad?" she asked as soon as the door clicked shut behind them.

Agent Hunt was standing just down the hallway; he gave her a pinched expression as though he had tried to stop her father from barging into her questioning, but Solomon Scot had proved too formidable an opponent. Though she knew and understood what Agent Hunt had probably had to put up with from her dad, he had screwed up royally in allowing him anywhere near her work.

"Hunt," she said, condemnation flooding her tone.

"I'm sorry," he moaned. "He came armed." He pointed to two men behind him who were carrying the telltale briefcases of well-paid lawyers.

Her spirit slipped, threatening to leave her body at the sight of the two suit-clad men. There was nothing she hated more than a sleazy defense attorney, unless it was two sleazy defense attorneys.

"I see you brought your henchmen. What did your men in there do that would require that level of defense?" she asked, nudging her chin in the direction of the lawyers.

"*They* didn't do anything they weren't paid to do." He put his hand on her shoulder. "If I was really upset, do you think I would have come down here myself? I would have just sent my men. I'm here to talk to you, to let you know that my team is not guilty of any wrongdoing in what transpired today. And if you wish to pursue any sort of legal action, it would be a foolhardy endeavor." He gave her the look, the same look he had given her as a child when the discussion was over.

Well, she wasn't a child anymore. She was almost thirty years old and well outside the realm of requiring her father's permission—especially when it came to her job. Nonetheless, that didn't mean he was wrong in his handling of the situation. If she was in his shoes and her company's name made it into headlines related to a shooting—since Troy and Mike worked for him through STEALTH—she would have brought along a set of lawyers as well.

His company, his reputation and her family's fortune depended on the business prospering.

"I have no intention of arresting your men. So far as I've learned, they are not the guilty party here. They did not pull the trigger, but I'm interested in why they were involved in a shooting. So far, they haven't given me any information."

Her father nearly cracked a smile, but it was so rare she wasn't sure she had actually seen what she thought she had seen flicker over his face. "They are under several NDAs that prohibit what and with whom they can speak. I'm sure you know all about them."

Just because his contractors had signed nondisclosure agreements didn't mean they could get out of this situation without filling in some critical details.

"I don't have a problem working around your NDAs, but I do need to get a positive ID on our shooter and make sure that nothing like this happens in Missoula again." She tried to stare her father down, but he didn't break his gaze. "If you have any idea who was up there, pulling the trigger, then you need to tell me. Right now."

Her father gripped her shoulder a little tighter and gave it a hard squeeze. "The person or group responsible for the shooting will not be caught. Not by you and not by me. You would be smart to just brush this event under the rug." He paused. "Now, I know you need to make a series of public statements and cross your *t*'s and dot your *i*'s, but I would request that you protect my teams and our family's company by keeping our names out of the headlines. Do whatever you need to do, but let's try to bury this as quickly and efficiently as possible."

She had a sickening feeling that her father was right. They wouldn't find this person. Her family's company, from what little she had managed to glean over dinners and overheard phone calls, had been taking military machining contracts for years. Once she'd heard talk of them building parts for a specialized aircraft that reportedly could be virtually "invisible" to their enemies.

She had a fair amount of acumen when it came to understanding some of the tech that was at America's disposal, but when it came to this, she felt out of her depth. And being out of her depth wasn't something she was accustomed to, and she didn't relish the sting it delivered. What she did know, with absolute certainty, was that her family now found themselves enmeshed in something with an odor to it.

Hunt appeared to be busy doing something on his phone and she stepped closer to her father so only he could hear what she said. "I will do what I can. Call it a professional favor. I'll pull my crews back on this, at least a little bit… Appearances." She glanced over her father's shoulder. Hunt seemed oblivious to their conversation, but she knew he was trying to listen in. "This can't happen again."

Her father nodded. "I will take care of things on my side."

It was the closest thing she could have gotten to a tacit admission that her father had a hand in today's events, and she hated it. She didn't like what was going on here, but she wasn't going to create a scene until she knew more.

She should have been dragging his ass into the interrogation room and having another agent working him over for answers, but with her father, that kind of thing never worked. This was hardly the first time he had found his feet in the fire. And even if she tried to get him to talk, all that would happen would be another swift end to any sort of questioning, thanks to his menagerie of lawyers.

"Will you please release them?" her father asked, motioning in the direction of Mike and Troy.

"They were never really being held. They could walk whenever they would have liked," she said, heading back into the interrogation room. Reaching into her pocket, she grabbed a business card and handed it to Troy. "If you need anything, let me know. Or if you think about anything that you can tell me that would stop this from happening again, I'm here."

Her father took the card from Troy's hands and ripped it in half, throwing the bits left of it down on the floor. "He won't be needing that. He has a job to do, a job that doesn't need FBI oversight. If I were you, I would make an effort to get things sorted with the public. And, from what I hear, you have something waiting from Agent Peahen. If I were you, I would jump."

Her chest tightened. How in the hell did her father know anything about what was going on in her inbox, her job? She tried to check any emotions from showing on her features. He couldn't know that he had gotten a reaction; if he did, it would be like blood in the water.

If it had been anyone else standing in front of her and pulling this kind of nonsense, they would have had their ass on the floor and their wrists in shackles. But no, not him, not the patriarch of her family, the man who cared for legacy and politics often to the detriment of the people he said he loved the most.

She could only imagine what he had gotten himself into, but she held no doubts that because of her family she was about to find herself swimming with sharks.

Chapter Eight

Troy sat outside of Kate's house for the second night in a row, staring at the yellow light that burned through the curtains of her front room. Occasionally a shadow would move by the window, teasing him with the flutter of the curtain. Tonight, he had sworn that he had almost seen her, twice.

He had looked into her just enough since the shooting to know she wasn't married, no kids and had graduated from Vassar with honors. Smart woman…driven woman…and perhaps she was the kind of woman who didn't want the tie-downs that came with a family. Or maybe she was the kind who was so myopically focused on her career that such things had never played a major part in her life.

Though he had sat outside of at least a hundred other houses in the dark in the middle of the night and watched over thousands of people, this was the first time he really felt uncomfortable. Yet, with a shooter on the loose, he couldn't ignore the nagging feeling that told him she was in danger, and that she needed him.

Or maybe it was the fact that he found her so goddamned sexy that bothered him the most. Generally, the people he watched were just put into one of two categories: high- or low-value targets. This time, his target didn't quite fit into either of those neat little squares.

He was too emotionally invested in this woman's welfare. There was nothing better than complete, abject dissociation when it came to emotions and specifically any sort of feeling that was registered in or near the heart. Both nights he had mulled over the whys of his being here, but it all came down to one thing—even if he never spoke to her again and she never knew that he was out here and patrolling for danger, that was okay. He would have done his duty. Hopefully nothing would happen, no shooter would show up in the middle of the night or bear down on her when she was leaving her house in the morning as she made her way to the federal building.

Hopefully he was making something out of nothing and she was completely safe. But, until he knew that this thing with the sniper was under control and in no way connected to her, he had to stay vigilant. STEALTH hadn't turned up anything of value yet, but it seemed awfully coincidental that the daughter of the owner of the company they were working for was at the scene of the shooting. In fact, the more he thought about it, the more he wondered if she was the sniper's target. Instead of waiting for Mike and him to drive by a random street, it made more sense the sniper had been staked out to catch action at the Bureau building.

He had to be the hero in the night, the hero that she never knew existed… He was her warrior, her guard, so she didn't have to stand alone.

This was who he had been meant to become. The keeper of the peace. The protector of the innocent. The man in the shadows.

Though he shouldn't have, he found himself smiling at the thought.

There was a flutter of the curtain as she must have breezed by. Things had been quiet in Kate's house for the last twenty minutes and the only other movement had been the flicker of her television. Besides the rustle of her curtains, everything seemed in order. It was nearly the time she normally shut down the downstairs for the night and made her way up to her bedroom. To a fault, her schedule was almost down to the minute. Predictability and patterns could be the downfall of even the best.

He tried to reassure himself that she would be fine, that the shooter probably wasn't coming after her, but with her jumping into the fight as she had— well, she had put herself into a new set of crosshairs: her father's. Who knew what her father would do to keep his secrets—secrets that not even Troy was completely privy to. As far as STEALTH and Zoey were concerned, he was on a need-to-know basis.

And, with ConFlux, that meant he was given the basic details and an objective.

He didn't mind working for Kate's father, Solomon Scot, but the man was one step from being a criminal, as far as he could tell. And yet many of the best and most profitable businesses he worked for were just that way. He didn't have qualms with people playing for keeps, particularly in the modern game of business that involved corporate espionage, dirty code, and terrorism at every level—especially in anything that involved health care, banking, insurance, government and military. Though those were the biggest players impacted in the corporate world, they were hardly an exhaustive list.

Cyber attackers loved to go after anything that showed a vulnerability, often with or without hope of financial gains. But in cases like the one with ConFlux, the company had more on the table and at risk than most in their field—thanks to their engineering, designing and machining.

He looked down at his phone as it vibrated on his wrist with a message. He had an email coming in from Zoey, nothing more than a status check. He needed to call her and let her know he was fine; no doubt she had been watching everything unfold. She'd made it no secret that she wasn't on board with his watching over Kate when his focus was supposed to be elsewhere, but she hadn't stood in his way, either. It probably helped that Zoey knew Kate. They ran in the same circles and played the same political games—more, both knew exactly how much could be at stake if this thing was poorly handled. It would be all their necks on the line if an innocent person, especially someone from the Bureau, turned up dead.

He couldn't stand the thought. Though he was more than aware he couldn't have any sort of feelings for the woman who was central to his being there, he couldn't help some of the fantasies that had moved through his mind. His personal favorite were the thoughts about what she liked in bed. When he'd met her, she'd seemed like the high-and-tight kind of woman, always in control… If he had to bet, she was probably the person in a relationship who was more of a pleaser. Maybe a bit more docile and less commanding, a bit of yin to the yang of her hard exterior.

The thought made his body come to life.

He had to think of anything other than her…the way her suit pants hugged her curvy hips… He could definitely take hold of those hips. Turn her around. Kiss the back of her neck as he pressed against her.

Stop.

He had to stop thinking about her.

This had to be the last night he was out here. No more. This being out here, thinking about her, it was all getting to be too much. Maybe he needed to call one of his brothers and have them take watch for a while. At least until he could get control back over his emotions. This emotions thing—there was a reason it wasn't his style.

Thankfully, Kate hadn't asked him a damn thing

about himself, his team or his family before her father arrived on scene and bailed his ass out. Though he was gifted at deflecting questions and at deception during interrogation, he wasn't sure that he could have maneuvered around Kate's questioning. There was something about her. Maybe it was the way she laughed, or the light in her eyes when she smiled, or maybe it was the softness that flecked her words when she talked to him, but there was something that made him want to open up to her.

There was a tap on the passenger's-side window. Kate stood, looking in. He sent her a guilty smile as he rolled down his car's window. How in the hell had she gotten the drop on him? "You know, if you are going to sit out here all night, you are going to need some coffee. Want to come inside?" She nudged her chin in the direction of her house.

"I have been told I'm good at surveillance. Thanks for proving all those people wrong," he said, with a nervous, uncomfortable laugh.

"You did fine. I'm just a little bit better than most when it comes to watching my six." She leaned into the car. She must have sneaked her ass out of the house and around him without noticing. He looked down the road in both directions. Just like him, she had obviously done more than her fair share of slinking around in the night, finding her way through the shadows.

"How long have you known I was out here?" he asked.

"My neighbor, old Mrs. Evans, called and told me that there was a guy watching my place the night after the shooting. Buddy, you're not in Kansas anymore. Here, the neighborhood watch has a few things to teach the Bu. I really thought you'd get bored and head out. How long are you planning on keeping this up?"

"Just until I know you are safe. Which, apparently, you are, thanks to old Mrs. Evans." He laughed, and his sense of ineptitude slipped away. In all honesty, he had gotten hold in his surveillance. Maybe a little part of him had wanted her to notice him, not that he would ever admit that to her…especially not the part about his sitting out here and letting his mind occasionally wander to a place in which he wondered what color panties she was wearing.

Thank you, nosy neighbor.

"Come on," she said, waving him out of the car as she made her way to the front door. "And if you are going to really watch someone, I would hope you would know that you should change out the model of car you drive once in a while."

He laughed, unbuckling his seat belt. "Oh, I will have to write that one down," he teased. "If you want to know the truth, I'm not getting paid to sit out here. This hunk of junk—" he pointed toward the old sedan "—is my personal vehicle. She ain't much, but in Missoula she *usually* blends in."

"She, eh?" She quirked her brow as she smiled at

him. "Why do I get the feeling that this is the only woman in your life?"

He wasn't quite sure what to make of her tone. There was a nuance to it that had him thinking that she was flirting with him or at the very least checking his relationship status, but he'd never been good enough with the opposite sex to read between those kinds of lines. He had to tread lightly and hope for the best on this one. "We are in a committed relationship."

She laughed, not giving anything away that he could read as she turned and made her way toward her front door. He followed her inside. Her house was typical of suburban Montana. It was a '70s-style two-story with a sunken living room and a bay window centering the wall. There was fresh carpet and new tile floors. The walls were covered in what looked to be a new coat of gray paint, and clean white baseboards adorned the floors. The entire place smelled like air fresheners and paint.

"How long have you been living here?" he asked, closing and locking the door. He glanced over at the pristine white couch in the center of the living room.

A true-crime show played on the television, but she barely seemed to notice.

She sighed as she slipped off her shoes and set them neatly on the floor beside the couch, then sat down. "Come on, now. You found where I live. You don't have to pretend like you didn't dig into exactly who I am and how I got to where I am."

There was a certain edge to her voice that made him wonder if there was some kind of past there beyond the stuff he already knew, but he wasn't sure he should press too much. The last thing he wanted to do was to make her clam up. He wanted her to be his friend…and who knew, maybe she would even take it easy on him and let him slip into her bed on an occasion or two. If he had to bet, she was probably wearing black panties. Cotton.

She leaned back, her breasts pressing against her shirt. He had seen her do that move once before, making him wonder if it was a concerted effort on her part to make him forget who and where he was and what he was doing.

And damn if it didn't work.

She was so beautiful.

"You get pretty much everything you want, don't you?" he asked, with a disarming laugh.

"What?" She giggled. "Why do you say that?"

"Really?" he asked, raising a brow.

She had to know how gorgeous she was, and he wasn't about to admit out loud that she turned him on. Nope, he was already out on a ledge by being here in her house. Zoey would have had a conniption fit if she knew where he was right now.

"I'm curious—are you going to tell me why you think I always get my way?" she pressed, a demure smile on her lips.

Jeez, she was going to give him a heart attack with

that smile. "You didn't tell your father I was here, did you?" he asked, trying to take the pressure off him.

Her smile disappeared. "Why would I do something that stupid?"

It wouldn't have been stupid of her to have let her father know about his surveillance. If anything, it would have been a predictable move. If he was her, he would have been digging around to learn everything he could about Mike and him and their roles inside her father's organization. And yet he had heard her father pull her off the shooter investigation. Did Mr. Scot really wield that much power over his daughter…enough for a few simple words to put a stop to a federal investigation?

If that was true, maybe he was barking up the wrong tree in attempting to get to know her a bit better.

Then again, he wasn't here to seduce her. If something happened between them, it would be only an added benefit. He tried not to look at her as she re-adjusted herself on the couch. Her smile, her laugh, her body were all driving him crazy.

He grumbled inwardly.

"So, you haven't told anyone that I'm here?" he asked, giving her a soft, inquisitive look that he hoped put her more at ease.

She shook her head. "Do I need to?" She paused. "From what little time we spent together, I didn't pick up on anything that made me think you were a danger to me. A danger to others…now, that is an entirely different thing. But me... I... You seem to have a soft spot. I mean, why else would you spend all that time outside of a girl's house, standing guard?"

"What the hell?" he asked, the words spilling from his lips like cheap wine.

Had he been that obvious?

Ugh. He could kick his own ass. Here he was, thinking he was so coy, maybe even edging on a little bit of Rico Suave, and yet...the slap of reality stung.

"You can try to deny it, but I have made a profession out of my ability to read people." She giggled. "Besides, it's not just every person I bring in for an interview who turns up at my house a few hours later."

"I wanted to make sure you were home, safe and sound. The shooter had to have gotten a bead on you. They have to know who you are. And even if they're not coming for you, you just never know if there are others out there who want to do you harm."

"I appreciate your concern. But are you watching my whole team? The shooter could have gotten a bead on them too." She smiled up at him and patted the couch beside her. "You don't think I thought about why and what would have brought you out here? To an address I didn't give you and I have worked hard to keep private?"

He took a sudden liking to the cuticle along the side of his thumb, picking away a nonexistent piece of skin.

"You don't have to be embarrassed," she continued. "I'm not upset. I'm impressed you found me. And I'd be lying if I didn't say I was a little flattered. My ex-boyfriend couldn't even bother to text half the time. Once, he was working in Japan for two weeks and I didn't hear a damn thing." She stopped talking and took a breath, making him wonder if she regretted sharing so much about her past. "It's nice to know someone cares enough about my welfare that they would go to such work to find me."

"Zoey pointed me in the right direction," he said, trying to downplay the exact thing he was glad she had noticed.

"So, she knows you are here?" She looked at him.

He nodded. "She wants to keep you safe almost as much as I do. Even if she thinks I'm overdoing it."

"As long as that is why you are really here." She narrowed her eyes. "Or did my father send you to watch me? To make sure I was doing as he ordered?"

He put his hands up in surrender, catching her gaze. "No, I promise you. He doesn't even know I'm here. And if he did…" He looked away, composing himself. "I'm not sure I would have a job when he was done with me."

There was an uncomfortable silence between them. He hadn't meant that her father didn't care about her welfare—far from it, if he had to venture a guess—but he didn't want to head down that conversation path when things had been going so well between them… Flirty, even.

"Uh," she said, searching for the right thing to

say…something that wouldn't brush against the tension that was filling the air of the room, he guessed. "Do you want something to drink? Sorry. I don't mean to be a bad host."

He laughed. "You weren't expecting me, so is it still considered hosting if I show up like a stray dog?"

"A stray dog? Is that what we call surveillance now?" She giggled as she walked toward the side bar between the kitchen and the living room. "Do you drink?"

"I haven't in a long time, not because I'm opposed, just too busy to carve time out." He rubbed his hand over the back of his neck. "Not to mention the fact that I don't bounce back from a night out like I used to."

She laughed. "Come on, now. You're not old. What are you, like, thirty-four?" She glanced over at him, no doubt looking for a smattering of gray at the temples or a few stray lines near the corners of his eyes.

"Ouch," he said, looking at himself in the mirror that was on the wall behind the couch. "Do I really look that old?" He ran his hands over the start of scruff that was building up on his chin. There were the starts of a few wrinkles here and there, but nothing that was super noticeable to a person who wasn't looking for them.

She grimaced, her nose doing this cute wrinkling thing that almost made him weak at the knees.

"Sorry. I guess I'm not as good as I thought… How old are you?"

He smiled over at her, and there was a little sparkle in her hazel eyes. "I'm thirty-three. I won't be thirty-four for a couple more weeks."

She reached over and playfully cuffed his arm. "Has anyone ever told you that you are a pain in the ass? You made me feel terrible!"

He laughed, feeling a tad bit evil but glad he had made her feel something. "You were close. And, yes, a great number of people have referenced that as one of my many character flaws."

"Oh, one of many, eh?" She raised a brow. "Is there a long list? Wine?"

He nodded and she took out a bottle from the rack and started to open it as he thought of all the things others liked to point out were wrong with him—one of his previous girlfriends had loved to remind him of how he was never there, even when he was in the same room. She wasn't wrong.

"Do you really want to know about me?" he asked, fidgeting with the side pocket on his tactical pants.

She cleared her throat as she uncorked the bottle with a heady pop. It was a welcome sound. "You don't have to tell me anything you don't want to. I was just thinking that you know much more about me than I do about you. I just have to even out our playing field."

"I didn't mean to make things awkward. I'm just surprised is all," he said, grabbing two glasses hanging from the side bar. He took the bottle from her and poured them each a glass, like he had done it a thousand times in her living room before. "I don't get asked a lot of questions. And I'm normally only around Mike. He's not much of a conversationalist. I guess I've just become a bit of a hermit."

She laughed, putting down the corkscrew and taking one of the glasses he offered her. "A bit of a hermit? Come on, now. You're one step away from living in a cave." She gave him a long sideways gaze that made his chest clench.

"Speaking of awkward and honesty, I've spent more than a night or two in caves around the world. Safest place you can be sometimes." He took a long drink of the wine, and he didn't taste anything other than the pasty flavor that came with being uncomfortably close to a beautiful woman whom he'd had more than a few dirty thoughts about.

Was it going to be one of *those* nights? He had to pull his act together.

"I shouldn't have come out here," he said, putting down his nearly empty glass. "I'll go."

"No." She touched his arm. He should have pulled away, but he remained still. "You don't have to leave. And, as luck has it, I like a little bit of awkward. Just promise me that next time you come to my house, you just knock on the door. You are welcome here." She slipped her fingers down his skin, leaving a fire behind, as she poured him a fresh glass. "As it so happens, I'm not much of a social butterfly, either."

"Do you think two introverts can make a good relationship?" he asked, taking his glass of wine.

"I do." She lifted her glass, sipping. "So, I'm assuming you're not married?"

"Only to my little car out there." He shrugged. "My job has been the kind where I am sent all over the world. I don't know when I'll come back. Doesn't make for great relationships. Phone calls and texts are a far cry from real intimacy. And the distance… It is rough when you both are living your own lives, lives that don't really include each other."

"What do you mean your job *has been* that kind of thing?" she asked, walking over to the couch and sitting down.

She hadn't run away when he'd admitted to his inability to commit, something he was glad to get out in the open. It was a good sign, but he hated to get his hopes up too much. "Recently, my job shifted from military-style operations into more of the corporate surveillance."

"Like what you are doing for my father?"

He joined her on the couch, being careful to give her space. "I don't really work directly for your father. My company is contracted for some *things* for his company, but I work for STEALTH."

"You know that is nothing more than semantics, right?" She moved and her knee brushed against his, making a fire race through him where they had touched. "And you made your position with my father and the effects of his wrath clear. So, why don't we cut the crap. Let's just be open and honest with each other. We are both cut from the same cloth, and as it is, we're going to have to either give all or nothing."

He ran his thumb up and down the stem of his glass, thinking about all the things he wanted to tell her, very few of which had anything to do with his job. "It's not that I don't want to be open. It's just… you have to know, just like you, secrets are my life. There are a million things I could never tell you and you will never be able to tell me."

And how could they build a friendship on that kind of quicksand?

In the end, it came to one decision: trust or get out.

He had already trusted her before. He had given her his job and his identity. For a man like him, who was still dark… If anything, it was stupid of him. And yet he had already made the leap of faith. What were a few more steps? She wasn't just some random person. She had gone through hundreds of hours of background checks and security clearances— possibly even more than him.

But he'd read too many reports and gone to too many classes to just ignore all the warning signs that came before opening up. What he was finding hardest to ignore were the feelings that filled him when he looked into her eyes, feelings that made him want to reveal more than just his professional background, but how the source of the dull ache in his heart seemed to ease when he was near her.

"I respect your need for privacy—you know I do," she said, sounding demure. She cleared her throat, like she was trying to shift the timbre of her voice from questioning to reassuring. "How much did you know about me when you took this job?"

He swallowed another drink, this time slower and more deliberate, letting the strawberry and moss flavors of the wine melt into his tongue. "Honestly, I knew your father had two daughters, but I didn't know much about you. Just the basics. And you can believe he didn't mention that you were working for the Bureau."

"Would it have made a difference if he had?" she asked.

He paused, thinking for a moment. "No. I don't think it would have. Normally, a corporate owner's family plays no role in my investigation unless they work for the company involved."

"I know you probably don't want to tell me, but you know I have to ask…"

He sighed, knowing the question even before it slipped from her lips. Didn't she know he was struggling in his attempt to stay quiet? "You know I can't tell you what I was hired to look into or why. That is between my company and your father and his board. But I can say that I don't think your father is looking for trouble. If anything, quite the opposite." Was that why she'd let him in, been acting so friendly—just to get this info?

She reached over and put her hand on his knee as a softness came over her features. "Thank you."

He stared down at her hand before he put his hand atop hers and gave it a light squeeze. "You're welcome. I can only imagine what you are going through right now, but you are taking all this like a champ. I'm impressed. I know it's hard when you are forced to face drama that surrounds your family, especially when it has the potential to affect your job and your standing in it."

"You're the strong one," she said. "You stood out there, under fire, and instead of running, you moved to cover the innocent."

He felt many things, especially with his hand on hers, but strength wasn't even close to the top of the list... In fact, all he could think about were his many weaknesses.

"I'm not strong. I'm well trained and it's my job to protect those who can't protect themselves." He pulled his hand from hers, regretting it as soon as her face fell.

Was it possible that she was as confused as he was? He veered from thinking she was interested in him to thinking she was interested only in what he could tell her about his work for her father.

They hadn't known each other long enough or well enough to find themselves in the situation they were in, but there was no denying there was something moving between them—and not the freak-in-the-sheet kind of thing. No, there was a deeper feeling than just mutual attraction. It was more like a deep understanding and respect.

Yeah, she was going to be dangerous to have in his life in any capacity.

He stood up and refilled their glasses, draining his and then filling it again, emptying the bottle. Though drinking wasn't their best option, when he was feeling the way he was toward her, staying sober was entirely too stressful. The last thing he wanted to do was be even more awkward than he already was.

Hopefully she had a thing for goofy dudes, dudes who didn't quite fit into any box and constantly found themselves at least three steps from normal.

"How deep does this thing with my father run? Are there people in the Department of Defense involved in his *stuff*, or is your involvement just a preventative sort of thing?"

He sucked on his teeth for a moment before he finally decided to answer. Maybe it was the slight buzz he was starting to feel or being near her, but he had to give her something she could work with—the more she knew, the more she'd be able to stay safe. "Preventative. Your father is doing what he can to take steps to keep anything from becoming a larger-scale problem."

"So, you're saying that he thinks there is someone in his company who is spying?" she asked, not bothering to beat around the bush.

He liked that she just jumped on his olive branch and tried to make it into a spear. "It's not about what he thinks or doesn't think—it's about what my team and I are able to prove. Zoey's digging deeper into the cyber side of things, but we're trying to find where the strong and weak points are in the organization."

She sent him a pointed smile. "You know, it would have been a lot easier if you had just told me all this from the beginning instead of making me pry it out of you." She took a sip of wine, and as she did, he could have sworn a faint redness took to her cheeks. "If I had to guess, your not wanting to tell me had more to do with the fact that you wanted to see me again than it did with your need for secrecy."

"Come on you know I have to protect my company's secrets. It can literally come down to life and death." As he spoke, the heady warmth of the wine slipped through him, filling him with reckless bravado. She wanted truth? He'd give it to her. "But I have to say, holding out until you and I have found ourselves here… It definitely was an added benefit. If I was a smarter man, I would have planned this out instead of merely falling ass first into it."

"You mean when I caught you lurking outside?" She paused for a split second. "And you can be as self-deprecating as you like, but we both know you're not a stupid man. If you were, you'd have had a damn short shelf life in the contracting world. Zoey doesn't allow for anything or anyone but the best."

"Zoey is tough." He gave her a sly grin as he reached over and took her hand. She didn't pull away and instead laced her fingers between his. This was all…so fast, and yet it felt so perfect. "And as for lurking, ouch, that's a little harsh. Don't ya think? I just wanted to make sure you had the highest level of security—call it tactical protection."

She leaned close, her breath caressing the side of his face as she whispered into his ear. "You can call it what you like, but I know why you are doing what you're doing. I know what you're feeling." She pressed her cheek against his.

In that moment, nothing else in the world mattered. There was only her and the way she felt pressed against him and how, with this oh-so-complicated touch, his world expanded.

Chapter Nine

Troy smelled like the inside of his car, an aroma of bar soap, protein bars and his clean-scented cologne. If someone had told Kate that this mixture of scents would be the greatest aphrodisiac she had ever experienced, she would have called them crazy. And yet here she was…her face pressed against his as she worked through all the feelings inside of her and how most were in direct competition with all the things she wanted to do with him and to his body.

Confused, there was only one thing that moved to the front of her mind, one thought, one need, one desire… She had to kiss him. To feel his lips pressed against hers. To hear the sound he made when her tongue skipped over the subtle ridges and valleys of his lips.

She grazed her thumb over the back of his, imagining what it would feel like to have his hands travel down her body as she kissed him. Would he know what she liked? Or was he the kind of lover who needed to be told what to do, to be trained in the art of pleasing her?

Troy seemed like the kind of man who was a bit uncomfortable around women, but that could have been the residual effects of his lonely job. And she wasn't one to judge when it came to sexual acumen. Sure, she'd been with a few men, but that didn't mean she was a sex expert.

She chuckled.

"Something funny?" he asked, leaning back and away from her touch.

The place where their skin had touched started to chill.

Why did I have to laugh?

One stupid thought and the greatest feeling she'd had in months had been stripped away from her. Why did she have to be such an idiot sometimes? Why couldn't she have played this whole thing with suave coolness?

Oh wait—she was a normal woman, that was why.

She sighed.

"You don't want to know what I was thinking," she said with a light chuckle.

If he knew the random thoughts that passed through her mind, he would probably head back out to his car, leaving only dust motes in his wake.

"If it makes you feel better, you and I were probably thinking about the same damn thing," he said, looking her square in the eye.

He had the most seductive green eyes, and gazing

into them was like standing in the heart of a Texas prairie in the middle of spring. There were so many different levels of the color, many she could have never imagined to be real.

She reached up and ran her hand over the stubble on his chin, her mind wandering from his words and settling back onto his features…the strong line of his jaw and the near ninety-degree line at its edge. Even his ears were in perfect proportion to the rest of his face… Her gaze drifted downward, toward his chest.

Before she could stop herself, her fingers twisted from his face, grazing over the soft cotton of his T-shirt and stopping just over his heart. It pulsed against her fingers. She put her palm down, feeling the quickening rumble as her hand cupped his perfect round pecs.

He flexed, smiling at her. "Do you like my moobs?" he teased.

She didn't just like them. "Given the right amount of invitation mixed with the correct amount of loosened inhibitions, and you know I would motorboat those things." She laughed, throwing her head back in joy.

He smirked. "Invitation? Hmm… I can't say that I've ever been asked if another person could motorboat my chest." He tapped his finger on his chin as if he was seriously contemplating the idea. "I'm flummoxed."

"Oh, did you just say *flummoxed*?" She laughed harder, her belly starting to ache. "You are cut off from any more wine."

"Don't be such a hater. There is nothing wrong with the word *flummoxed*. My grandfather loved that word."

"The fact that your grandfather loved it should be reason enough for you to leave that one in the past." She giggled, looking up at him from under her eyelashes.

He reached up and took her hand, which was still resting over his heart. "I haven't laughed this hard in a long time," he said. Lifting her hand to his lips, he gave her fingers a soft, tender kiss.

She could have died in that moment and considered her life well lived.

Of course, as if she had called down the wrath of the karma gods, her phone rang. It vibrated on the table in front of the couch just inches from their knees, repeating its angry buzzing like it was a hornet stuck behind a piece of glass.

He let go of her, and her hand drifted to her lap.

"You probably need to answer that," he said, motioning to her phone but seeming to respect her privacy enough not to grab it and hand it over to her.

The simple action, or inaction, made her think about what they would be like if they were a couple. She could almost imagine a Friday night, him going out to take down a company while she dug into crime-scene photos and tried to develop timelines for murders.

"Probably a robocall. Get lots of those."

The phone stopped its hornet dance and she relaxed back into the couch, hoping that they could pick up where they had left off, but not knowing exactly how she should start again.

"So, tell me more about your family. I know you said you have brothers…" she started.

The cute little smirk of his, the one that always seemed to appear when she did something slightly inept, reappeared. "I'm one of six kids. I'm the third in line to the throne, right ahead of Mike."

She was a bit surprised that he hadn't tried to put her off when she'd asked about his private life. "All boys?"

He shook his head. "Nah, five boys and a girl." He shrugged. "My parents were saints and possibly highly confused. I can't imagine raising six kids, not to mention six highly energetic and trouble-seeking children. We were *the worst.*"

"I can only imagine. I am one of two girls and we were bad…but six… Ouch."

He chuckled. "Both my parents worked full-time, which meant we were all on our own, for the most part. AJ, my oldest brother, tried to keep us in line, but most of the time he was the ringleader more than anything else."

"Oh yeah?" she asked, not wanting to stand in his way of opening up to her.

"Christmas was when we seemed to all be at our finest. There was nothing more fun than lining up the glass bulb ornaments and pinging them off with a BB gun." He laughed as he spoke, the words spilling out between chuckles. "I'm telling you, our parents should have quit at one… But my mother was an angel, seriously. She never mentioned a damn thing about all the missing ornaments. And I'm sure, though we tried to clean and hide the evidence after our target practices, she had to have known what we were up to when she had to buy new ornaments each and every year."

She laughed, but it was just as much at him and the joy in his face as it was for the craziness she was sure had taken place within his family. "I bet they got cheaper over time. You're lucky she didn't start buying the unbreakable plastic ones just to mess with you guys."

"If they would have been a thing back then, I'm sure she would have." He was laughing, but there was a whisper of sadness in the sound. "She was a great woman. Both of my parents were."

Kate stopped laughing. "I'm so sorry. How long have they been gone?"

"They've both been gone a couple of years now. They died on Christmas Eve in a car accident." He ran his finger over the glass. "They lived in Renton, near Seattle—where we all grew up. They were coming to Montana to spend the Christmas with me, Mike and Elle. We were all just starting our jobs with STEALTH. They were hit by a semi on Snoqualmie Pass. Died instantly."

"Holy crap, Troy… I can't even… I'm so, so very sorry." She couldn't even imagine the pain that must have come with that kind of traumatic event. She had thought dealing with her mother's breast cancer had been hard, but thankfully her mother had survived.

She didn't have the corner on the market when it came to hardship and suffering. If anything, his history was hands down more heart wrenching. All of a sudden, she felt entirely too sober, but she was grateful that he was finally giving her a piece of himself. He was starting to make a bit more sense.

But not why he had chosen to go into governmental contracting work. It wasn't a job that most could do. It was a job that was often not regulated, which made it like the Wild West and him a cowboy.

"Why did you choose to become a contractor? Was it because of the loss of your parents?"

"No, that happened after I was already training for STEALTH. I had been working as a contractor for a few other companies before that. I liked the work. I guess I got into the work because I was such a free-flying kid. We all went into contracting. In fact, my siblings and I all work for STEALTH."

That was amazing. One contractor in a family could be hard on the entire dynamic, thanks to the secrets, the going black and the disappearances out into the world for sometimes *years*…but six? Damn.

Maybe it worked better because they all lived in the same world and all worked for the same company. It had to allow them more candor when it came to the work they did. Maybe it was the best way to keep a family together.

"I haven't heard of a whole lot of female contractors. Especially when it comes to working out in the Sandbox. How does your sister like it?"

"She is far tougher than I am."

She nibbled at the corner of her lip. "What about the sexism?" Her thoughts moved to Agent Peahen… and all the work that would be waiting for her in the morning. It still rankled that her father had urged her to work with the man. She knew her dad had a lot of connections, and his reference to Peahen meant the agent had probably complained about her to her father. How petty.

She tried to ignore the gnaw of guilt that fluttered through her as she considered all the things she needed to do, but for once she could take a night for herself. It was terrible, but it had been entirely too long since she'd had a man in her house, not to mention edging in on her feelings.

"My sister doesn't open up to me a lot about the way men treat her, but I know it can't be easy. There aren't many women who get into contracting, for a reason. And as much as I would love to support having women in every role in the different teams, it would be really hard. There are places in the world where they just can't do what I do. They would end up dead."

She bristled. "Are you saying that you don't think women should be contractors?"

He shook his head, hard. "That's not what I'm saying. There are certainly jobs they are better at

than men. Women can get into places that I can't. Fe-
males are an asset…and a detriment… But the same
can be said about men. It's just about using the right
people for the right job. And when a higher-up gets
it wrong…it can be a real problem. Or if they get a
team that doesn't work cohesively together… Yeah,
no. It's bad news." There was a strangled sound to
his words, a noise between deep anger and heartache, as though he was trying to hold back emotions
that threatened to break through his stoic dam and
flood into his voice.

There was something there, something that rested
right below the surface, but she wasn't sure whether
or not she should push him for answers. It was better
to have things happen naturally, if they were meant
to happen at all.

"I quit the Sandbox a couple of years ago, you
know…after an attack. I had broken the rules. It cost
me."

"I'm sure you didn't do anything that bad. You
seem like such a good man," she said, gripping his
hand with hers.

"It wasn't about me being a good man…or a bad
man. It was about me making the wrong decisions."
He paused and slipped his hand from hers, patting
it as he stood up and moved away from her. "I got
into a relationship that was ill-advised. I loved her…
And it was that love, our relationship, that ended up
costing her the ultimate price."

She didn't know what to say. "I'm sorry" seemed

too feeble a response to the pain he was so clearly feeling when he spoke about the woman he had loved. So, she said nothing in hopes that it would respect whatever it was that was going on inside of him.

"We were hit with an EFP. She took shrapnel straight to the heart." He leaned against the side bar, putting his arms over his chest. "Her death, without a doubt, was my fault. I will have to live with the guilt of that knowledge for the rest of my life."

The guilt he was feeling was likely not his to bear, but there was nothing she could say that would assuage what he was feeling. Right now, all he needed was to be heard. And, if that was all she could do to make him feel better, she was willing to sit there and be the ear he obviously so desperately needed.

"I know, logically, that I didn't put that EFP out there. I couldn't have known it was there, or that it was coming for us, or that it would have hit the up-armored unit just right…but if I had stopped things before they had gotten serious, she wouldn't have been out there. She probably would have taken a transfer out of the hellhole. She would probably be the one working for STEALTH now, not me."

"So, you have survivor's guilt too?" she asked, her words soft and nonjudgmental.

He ran his hands down over his face. "I don't know why I told you all this. Needless to say, if I ever went to therapy, I'm sure that they would have a field day. I put the *fire* in *dumpster fire*."

She didn't agree. Not in the slightest. "You are just a man with wounds. It comes with the territory."

"Of being alive." He finished her thought, a thought she wasn't going to say.

"I'm sorry for taking things here," he said with a sigh. "I was rather hoping things between us would go a bit of a different direction… Though, now I'm not so sure that's a good idea—with me being the grim reaper and all."

She chuckled, though she shouldn't have. In moments like this, when darkness loomed heavy, the only thing that could make it all okay was levity. "Does the grim reaper have a sidekick?"

He looked at her, surprise and relief marking his features. "You know, I never thought about that. Maybe his sidekick would be his scythe."

"Not my favorite nickname, but it's still kinda badass, Grim."

"We may be among the strangest friends on the planet," he said, laughing.

He had called them friends… They were steadily moving in the direction she had wanted while still staying safely behind the line of a relationship. They could toe the line, but she would have to play it safe when it came to him.

She had to keep this professional, or at least try to. He was work, or at least he had to appear to be only a part of her work to the outside world. And that was to mention nothing about what her bosses within the Bureau would surmise. If they found out that the target of the shooting was sitting in her living room drinking wine, there would definitely be an internal investigation. Oh, and Peahen would have a field day when he heard about her unprofessionalism—he already had a chip on his shoulder.

"There is nothing I like more than to exist in the world of the strange, the dark horse and the odd ducks. We are the ones who keep the world fresh, away from the habitual monotony that comes with simply surviving. I've always wanted more than that. It's how I found myself doing what I'm doing. I never thought about it in grim terms, but I really do love being the scythe when it comes to cutting down evil."

"I know that feeling," he said, a tenderness that looked very similar to adoration upon his features. "We really would make one hell of a team."

There was a knock on the door, making her jump.

Who would be knocking on her door this late at night? For a moment, they sat in silence. Troy's hand was on his sidearm, and as she looked to him, he pressed his finger to his lips and silently roll-walked toward the bay window that looked out and onto the front porch.

He slipped behind the curtain, moving so he could make out whoever was standing at the door. As he looked, his hand moved from his weapon and his body relaxed from his action-ready tightness. "It's one of your friends from the Bureau," he said, shrugging as though he wasn't completely sure. "Older guy, maybe midfifties. Looks like he's driving a black Suburban, someone else is in the passenger side, but they are parked right in front of your place. They aren't trying to be covert, that's for damn sure."

Then he wasn't talking about Agent Hunt, who was just moving into his early forties.

Who else from the Bureau would show up on her doorstep in the middle of the night? The phone call… What if it had been Raft, the special agent in charge for her division? Her stomach dropped. She moved to ask Troy to leave the room and stay out of sight, but as she looked to where he had been standing, he was already gone.

He must have known what was at stake for her as well. She'd have to thank him later.

The door opened without a sound. Standing on the doorstep was Agent Peahen. Fury roiled through her. "What in the hell are you doing here? You didn't seriously drive here all the way from Billings, did you?"

Peahen's face puckered, his lips pulled into the closest thing to a sneer without actually being one. Their distaste for one another was mutual. "Thanks for the warm welcome."

"Why are you on my doorstep?" she asked.

Had there been some kind of informational breach in which everyone in the effing world had suddenly been informed of her address? If Peahen had found her, it was time to move again.

"I wouldn't be on your doorstep if I didn't have to be. And yet here I find myself." Peahen grumbled something she couldn't quite make out. "I'm here for the files you promised me. You have access to them, correct? I'm not leaving here until you have forwarded them all to me."

"Why do you care so much about a burglary that happened five years ago?" She tried not to sound as annoyed as she felt. She never had sent him those files, mostly because she'd not wanted to jump when he ordered her to. And because her father had mentioned it as well.

"What do you care? You didn't solve it."

Kate gritted her teeth in an attempt to keep from taking him down with a quick two-finger jab to the throat. "Has there been another burglary, something you think may be tied to the case? Or are you reopening the investigation for another reason?"

He groaned, leaning his head back, as if the mere fact she had questions before she blindly handed her case over was out of line. "Look, I don't have to answer your questions. I'm not here to be interrogated. Now, you can give them to me willingly, or I will go over your head—in fact, you're lucky I haven't already done that."

The fact that he was standing on her doorstep, threatening her with going above her head, was odd. He'd already done this—told her he'd go to her superiors. Why hadn't he by now? Billings was a hell of a drive from Missoula. It certainly wasn't on his way to anything, at least not that she could think of.

"Peahen, I've no problem giving you the files. I have them with me. But before you do anything, I need to know why you need them and what you're actually doing here in Missoula." She gave him a critical look. "And don't give me any of that *I'm not here for an interrogation* nonsense. You can't expect me to just give you files, without asking a few questions. You are not that kind of friend, and you know it."

He snickered. "For someone that is inept at her job, you sure ask a lot of questions. Maybe if you treated your suspects the same way you're treating me, you would break a lot more cases."

Her hands balled into tight fists. No one would think anything of her slugging him if they had been there to hear what he was saying. "You're one to judge, Peahen. The last time I checked, I actually have a higher prosecution rate than you do."

"Fine." Peahen turned to leave. "You are going to regret the fact you're being such a little… Well, so *unprofessional*. And when your dad hears how you treated me, you're going to get it from every side. You deserve whatever consequences come your way. Whether you want to admit it or not, we fight for the same team."

"Stop right there," she said, charging out the door after Peahen. "My father mentioned you the other day and now you're mentioning him. What the hell is going on with you two? Did you have something to do with the shooting in Missoula the other day? Is that why you're here?"

"Not that it's any of your business, but I had a meeting in town. I was just getting back from Salt

Lake City and the regional headquarters. It was easier just to come over here and take care of it in person."

She wasn't sure if she believed him or not. Yet
there was something to his voice that made her think
he was telling the truth. He wasn't displaying any of
the typical signs of deception, but that didn't mean
anything, considering he knew just as well as she
did what those signs were. He could have easily been
trying to deceive her.

"And what about your ongoing *friendship* with
my father?" she asked.

Peahen sniffed, annoyed. "Your father and I go
way back, long before you even joined the agency."

She'd had no idea. In fact, her father had never
mentioned a connection with Peahen before this
week. Had Peahen been part of the reason that she
had been picked up by the agency? The thought pet-
rified her. For her security clearances, there was no
doubt in her mind that they had looked into her and
all the people connected to her. Peahen had to have
been asked about her, and the fact that she was currently an agent meant that he had to have said something to her credit.

The possibility that he had done her a favor without her even knowing it still didn't make up for what
a jerk he was every time she had dealt with him over
the last five years.

For a moment, she considered asking him into the
house, but she glanced over her shoulder in the direc-

tion of where Troy had been standing. If Peahen got nosy, or turned down the wrong hall, he very well could end up face-to-face with Troy. She didn't need them in the room together.

"Let me go grab my phone, and I'll send in the files. I want you to promise me that you'll keep me up-to-date with your findings on this case."

"That's fine," Peahen said.

She jogged back up the steps and to the living room. Grabbing her phone, she made her way back outside.

Peahen look slightly less annoyed than he had five minutes ago, but only slightly. He wore the same pinched expression he always did, making her wonder if that was just his face. If he was married, she felt sorry for the woman.

After a few searches through her files, she sent off the email. "It should be in your inbox."

"Great." Peahen's lips quivered into what she assumed was almost a smile. "And, believe it or not, your dad is a good man. You should take it easy on him and me…once in a while." With that, he turned and strode away, obviously not waiting for her to say anything in return.

A tightness she hadn't realized she'd been experiencing in her chest loosened. She'd never believed anything Peahen had ever told her, but it could have been their acrimonious personalities at fault rather than any particular transgression toward one another. His evaluation of her father, and the fact Peahen had acted in favor of her in the past... Well, it changed things.

And though her father was by no means a perfect man, it was good to know he wasn't evil or corrupt— at least she assumed.

She loved him and her mother, and they had done much to show her love when she was a child.

When she'd been younger, she had been studying the violin. Twice a year for what must have been fifteen years, she had performed in recitals. During high school, she had played with the Missoula Symphony as the youngest first chair. She'd played with them for four years before she had gone to Vassar. Her parents had never missed a single performance, not even when her mother had been diagnosed with breast cancer and had been seeking treatment.

It was strange, but after what had happened the other day, those memories and their support had started to lose their texture, like someone had started to pull at the strings that wove together to make her soul. In essence, it was as if her father's possible complicity in the shooting had made her question everything—even who she was.

And here she was, back in that same confusing reality in which she didn't know who or what was the driving force in her life—and all thanks to a five-minute meeting with a man she had thought was her enemy.

She made her way back inside. After—well, *if*— Troy went home, she would have to dig deeper into the old burglary case. There was something that they were all looking for, and she had a feeling that it went far deeper than she had initially assumed.

The house was silent as she closed the door behind her. "Troy, you can come out now. Thank you for what you did back there. It would have been hard to explain why you are here." She paused, waiting for Troy to answer. There was no response.

Making her way around the house, her heart sank as she realized that Troy was gone.

Chapter Ten

He shouldn't have just left Kate like that last night, but in the moment, he hadn't known what to do. All he had known for sure was that, for her sake, he couldn't be seen in her house or anywhere near her property. After he'd alerted Kate to the BuCar outside her house, he had slipped out the back and around the block. When he'd gotten into his car and driven away, the last thing he had seen was Kate running out after Agent Peahen.

Troy had worked with Peahen once before on an investigation out of Billings, and it hadn't been one of his favorite assignments. The agent had thought himself far above him, both intellectually and morally, and had made it clear. If he'd worn a general's uniform beneath the suit, Troy wouldn't have been surprised.

If he had added himself to the mix, there was no way Kate would have come out unscathed. Not with Agent Peahen on the warpath. There was no telling what he would do—he definitely didn't need any more artillery, and especially none in the form of an agent mixing business with pleasure.

Not that there was any real pleasure between him and Kate. Sure, they had flirted. They had even held hands and touched one another in ways that were definitely more than two friends...but that didn't mean they had gone beyond the point of no return, did it?

He looked over at the clock beside his bed— 9:00 a.m. There wasn't anyone moving outside of his bedroom at the STEALTH headquarters, located on the Widow Maker Ranch. Everyone was probably already buzzing around their day, getting things done. He shouldn't have slept in so late. Zoey was supposed to call him in twenty minutes and he needed to be on his game when she did. No doubt, she would ring ten minutes early. She lived on the Anglo system of time—if a person was on time, they were ten minutes late.

It had been tough getting used to everyone's quirks when he had set foot back on American soil. Civilians, and even contractors who had never been in the military, were of an entirely different mindset than he was.

One of his friends, Jesse, had worked at his side and gone through training with him and finally into the same unit. Jesse went on to marry a woman and have four amazing kids, but even now when on the phone together, they would frequently admit that no one understood them better than they understood one another. They were brothers. No, deeper than brothers… Mike didn't even understand him as well as Jesse did.

Jesse had been with him when Tiff had been killed. That alone—that moment of horror—solidified a bond that was already stronger than diamonds or blood.

Maybe he should call him. At the very least, Jesse would tell him he was being a fool when it came to Kate, and maybe he could get his head straight. He hadn't been this screwed up when it came to a woman since, well…he would say Tiff, but even their relationship wasn't this unnavigable.

Then again, what was there to ask? He imagined exactly how the conversation would go down: "Hey, man, I think I'm falling for a woman who I'm helping to solve a shooting… Yeah, the dude was trying to take out Mike. Yeah… Her family owns the company I am investigating."

Jesse would tell him to tuck and roll, and get the hell out of the country as fast as humanly possible. It wasn't even worth the breath to ask him his opinion. Jesse was always of the rational frame of mind. The mind that rarely deferred to the heart.

Regardless of what he felt, wanted or yearned for, he needed to concentrate on the task at hand. And he needed to apologize for his sudden departure. Kate probably wasn't the kind of woman who was wondering about his welfare, but she did seem like the kind of woman who didn't appreciate anyone sneaking out of her place.

When he'd been helping her with the wine, there

had been a picture on the wall beside the side bar. In it, Kate had been standing with her mother and father and what looked like her boyfriend...or past boyfriend. He'd dug around, but the internet was devoid of any sort of current information. She definitely wasn't a publicity junkie in either her public or her private life. It was great for her, but it made it more of a challenge for him when it came to investigations. Like most agents, she kept her social-media presence scant and locked tight.

His phone rang. Zoey. "Hello?" he answered.

"Are you happy?" Zoey wasn't much of one for hellos. Or goodbyes.

"Happy about what?" he asked, not sure based on her tone if he should find a bomb shelter before she continued her rant or if he should purge his soul to her.

She sighed, now definitely annoyed. "Are you done watching over your girlfriend?"

Oh.

"What do you need from me?" he asked, taking the high road instead of getting hooked by her emotionally hijacking statement.

"Oh, so you are ready to get back to work. I'm glad to hear it." Zoey's tone dulled. "I need you to go back to the ConFlux building. You need to see if you can't hack into their system through their Wi-Fi— it's their weakest point. Then I will take care of the rest. After you are done with that, I need you to see if you can infiltrate the building without setting off any alarms. You have whatever resources you need to make this happen."

"Has there been any evidence that someone has been breaching their networks? Their building?"

"Not that they have divulged, but there is something going on. Solomon expressed concern that there may very well be someone trying to run a copy code on their servers, as there has been information in the past which has now gotten into the wrong hands. I asked him if anything new had been leaked, and he didn't believe so."

Troy made his way to the kitchen, took out a travel mug and poured himself a cup of coffee. "Which means that it isn't a hacker issue… At least, I wouldn't think so. If things are only going missing sporadically, this sounds like a personnel problem or someone from within their IT department—but you and I have talked about this before."

"Before the shooting, yes." Zoey paused. "Which is part of the reason I thought I needed to call and talk to you. I just got a ping on our shooter. I don't have a confirmed identity, but I worked the known cell phone signals in the area against the buyers and sellers of that make and model of rifle and rounds. Then I went through the information I pulled, and there is a short list of possibilities—three potential suspects. Two are still in the area."

"Who is the third?"

"The third person on our list… Well, that's the tricky part. I don't think this person would have had

anything to do with this. Not with their clearances."
There was the sound of a pen clicking in the background as Zoey spoke, her nervous tic.

Whatever name she was about to give him—it was going to be good.

"I know we are probably at a dead end with this one, but it's a special agent named Aaron Peahen."

Troy spit out his coffee. "You have to be freaking kidding me. It really isn't funny."

"What?" Zoey asked. "I'm not messing with you. Why would you think I was? You know this guy?"

"Yeah, I saw him last night. You said he was the only one on your list who hasn't been using the Missoula cell towers, but I know for a fact that he was here at least within the last twelve hours."

There was the click of key strikes. "According to what I'm seeing here, he appears to be in Salt Lake City."

"When?"

There was more tapping. "He has been there ever since the shooting. At least according to his SIM card."

He shook his head. Peahen was a jerk, but he was still an agent. He'd gone through nine months of background checks before he'd even been able to go to Quantico to train to be an agent. This was not their shooter. He wouldn't be a trigger puller, not in any sort of situation. He was closer to the kind of person who would be a computer jockey.

"That probably has something to do with whatever

is going on at the FBI." His thoughts went straight to Kate. There were pieces missing in the puzzle, pieces that revolved around her, but he just couldn't imagine what exactly locked these things together. "There is no way that Peahen is our guy. He's an uptight dude who gets his jollies making people say 'how high' when he barks out 'jump.' Not the type to go haywire with a gun. Send me the info you have on the other two. I'll get to work."

"Will do." Zoey clicked away. "As for the other guys on my list, they are both current employees of ConFlux."

"And you didn't think that they were more likely to be our shooters than a verified *good guy*?" Troy scoffed.

"You and I both know that there is no such thing as good guys and bad guys. We are all human. We all screw up. We all hurt the people around us. We all occasionally make crappy decisions. It's part of the gig."

"Yeah, but two employees of the company we are investigating? These are our bad guys. One of them, at least."

"It's possible, thus why they are on my list. But these two, neither have any sort of record of violence or training with weapons."

"But you said that they had access to the right kind of ammunition and rifle. But neither shoots?" Nothing about this rang quite right.

"One, Chris Michaels, is married to a woman who

is a major in the army. She had bought a rifle similar to the one used. There was no serial number on the sniper's weapon. But we're having a team go over it to see if it was scratched out. Definitely could have been her gun. You look into it."

"On it. I'll send Mike over to their address. As long as they don't have an electronic lock gun safe, he should be able to make quick work of it and gain access to their guns and let us know if her new acquisition is missing—if it is, then it's possible she or her husband is our sniper." STEALTH operated without search warrants, and he knew his brother could get a look at that gun, if it was there, by staying just one millimeter over the right side of the law. He took a sip of his coffee as he tried to work through all their leads. "But we may be dealing with someone who had the armory skills to fabricate or build their own weapon. It would be what I would do if I was the one up there pulling the trigger, knowing I'd have to leave my weapon behind. I'd need to take a closer look at the weapon, though, and the FBI has it now."

He clicked on his email and scrolled until he found Zoey's latest. He opened it up. There were three images of the photos of each of their possible suspects and three PDF files with all applicable background information. First, he opened the photo of Peahen, likely the one that was from the Bureau, and his badge. The second, Chris Michaels, looked like a man who could hold his own in a bar, Jack Reacher style.

"And what about this third guy? Sal Baker?" The

man staring back at him from his cell phone was in his midthirties, fit, and professional looking with a black pin-striped suit.

"The possibility of him being involved in this is all low, but he is worth checking out." Zoey paused, probably pulling something up as she talked to him. "From what I have, his nose is clean. No history of anything remarkable. Just a typical nine-to-fiver."

"With a penchant for high-powered sniper rifles?" he asked.

His phone beeped with another call. Glancing down, he saw a restricted number pop up on his screen. "I got to go. I'll let you know what I find."

"Roger that," Zoey said, hanging up without an-other word.

He liked that about her; she definitely didn't waste a whole lot of time when it came to chitchat.

"Hello?" he asked, pressing on the other call.

"Come to your door." Kate sounded strange, rigid.

He walked out of his bedroom. The place was a mess, with clothes hanging over the back of a chair and work shoes pitched exactly where people had taken them off and flopped down in their chairs.

As he walked toward the door, the ranch dog, Chuck, bounded out from the back bedroom. "Oh hey, buddy." He gave the chocolate Lab a scratch be-hind the ear and was answered with a quick nibble of the fingers and a lick. "I see how it is, you snot. You don't care about getting up with me in the morning, but as soon as a hot woman shows up at the door, you're racing to go."

Chuck answered with a lolling tongue and a wag of the tail as he trotted to the door. There was a tap on the door and the dog started to prance from one foot to the other as he worked out excited circles.

"Yep, all you care about is the chicks." Troy laughed as he made the dog move back so he could open the door. "It's okay, bud. I feel exactly the same way."

Kate was standing on the front porch, her back to the door as if only moments before she hadn't knocked to remind him that she was still there. Was she as nervous to be here as he was to see her?

"I would ask how you found me, but I think I know," he said.

She turned around and he expected to see her smiling at him, or even maybe mad, but he didn't expect what he saw... Kate had been crying. Her eyes were red and bloodshot, and she looked like she hadn't slept since the last time he had seen her.

"What in the hell is going on? Are you okay?" His words came out in a rush.

She nodded. "I'm fine." Her voice was raspy and hoarse from what he assumed was a night spent crying. "I got some bad news a couple hours ago."

"Babe, what? What happened?"

"It's my father..." she said, the words sounding more like sobs than real words.

He walked over to her and wrapped his arms

around her, holding her against his chest. Her body rattled with sobs as she let herself escape into his embrace.

"What happened?"

Her words were muffled, but he understood them just as well as if she had shouted them. "Someone… shot him. In his office. They murdered him."

Chapter Eleven

At her mother's house a little while later, Kate learned her mom had been calling every relative in her phone since she had found out about her husband's death. She told Kate she wanted to notify as many people as possible and to ask them not to speak to reporters or officials. But Kate knew the real reason for the busywork. It was so her mother could concentrate on a task instead of the pain that they were all feeling.

Her sister was flying in from Denver on the afternoon flight and would be touching down tonight. She hadn't taken the news well.

But then she couldn't blame her. She had gone to pieces when she learned about her father's death. She shouldn't have gone straight over to Troy's residence, but it was the only thing she could think to do after she had gotten over her initial shock.

She glanced over at Troy, who was busy making hot tea in the kitchen, complete with a tray of cream, sugar and lemon. She didn't even know her mother had lemons in the house and yet Troy had somehow found them.

Troy really was remarkable. He was unexpectedly chivalrous, kind and surprisingly open for a man who declared himself antisocial. If she hadn't known better or he hadn't told her, she would have actually thought he almost liked the general public. If she told him that, he would have some kind of snarky rebuttal.

He made his way out of the kitchen to them carrying the tray of tea and set it on her mother's marble end table. Her mother barely noticed.

In the past, her mother had been overly protective of the Carrara marble table specially imported from Italy. It was one of her most prized possessions, and the fact that she didn't seem to care now that someone put something on it that could potentially mar the gleaming white-and-gray surface was more shocking to Kate than her mother's sudden manic need to reach out to family.

"Troy, why don't you set that over here," she said, pointing toward the alabaster dining table in the adjoining room.

He picked up the tea set and followed her out of the living room, like an obedient member of her mother's household staff.

"Are you sure she's going to be okay?" Troy asked, motioning toward her mother.

In all honesty, she wasn't sure. Her mother had been through a lot with her breast cancer and forced retirement from the company, but she hadn't had to face that alone. Everyone in the family had surrounded her with love and understanding. Kate had even made a point of driving her mom to each and every one of her chemo appointments. Her mother had never really thanked her, but she hadn't expected her to.

Once her mother's cancer had gone into remission, Kate had assumed things would go back to normal and she would go back to work for the company, but she had become a woman who luncheoned.

It was as if her mother had decided after her illness that she was no longer going to devote herself and her life to the family business. She could only imagine how poorly that would have gone with her father had her mother made her intentions clear. Instead of telling him anything, so far as Kate knew, her parents had never addressed her mother's personality shift. It was as if her father had accepted it as part of the healing process.

Though he had seemed unaffected by it, when she and her sister had both declined his offer of going to work for ConFlux, he had blown up at both of them. So much so that her sister had stopped coming for Christmas and all major holidays for two years. It wasn't until she had gotten pregnant that she had finally come back to the family's fold.

No doubt, Julie was feeling terrible now, thinking about all the time she had lost with their father because their life plans didn't align.

And now who was going to take over the company? Her mother was the largest stockholder after her father's death. This would put her mother right back into the middle of the company's affairs.

"Here, have some tea. You need to focus on staying hydrated," Troy said.

It was quite the contradiction, this burly man handing her tea while he uttered the least manly thing he probably could have said.

The thought made her smile, the first real one all day. That he could bring her cheer, even in a moment like this, had to mean something, didn't it?

Her mother finally hung up the phone and walked into the dining room. She was wearing a white Dior suit with a blue Armani shirt beneath. It all complemented her platinum gray hair perfectly and Kate doubted it was by accident.

Perhaps her mother was already coming to accept that she was going to be a key player in ConFlux and had already started to dress the part.

"Your aunt Coraline is going to be flying in on Friday. Of course, she's going to bring her little dog, and if he pees on my floor again, she's going to have to attend another funeral service," her mother fumed.

"Oh my goodness, Mom, don't say things like that," Kate said, peering over at Troy to see if he had heard her mother's rant.

He was pretending to fuss with the teapot, lifting the lid and peering inside like he wasn't the one who had made the tea.

She appreciated his attempt to appear unobtrusive and spatially unaware.

"You know I was only kidding around. If we don't joke around about these things, then they tend to get so *emotional*. The last thing your father would have wanted would have been for us to shut down, get morose and stop working." Her mother's voice was high-pitched, almost frantic, as if she were fighting a battle for control, and she waved Kate off, as if she was nothing more than a nuisance. "Right now, the best thing we can do to honor Solomon and his legacy is to push through the heartache."

Troy poured her a cup of tea with sugar and lemon and handed it to her. "Here, that should make you feel better."

Her mother looked at Troy, seeming to notice his presence for the first time since they had arrived. "Who are you?"

"Mother, I already introduced you—"

"It's fine." Troy stiffened and stood up tall and straight as he extended his hand. "Mrs. Scot, I'm Troy Spade, a friend of your daughter's."

"A friend?" her mother asked, giving her a side-long glance to gauge exactly the depth of her and Troy's *friendship* as she shook his proffered hand.

"Yes, Mom, my work colleague. He is helping me on a case and was there when I received the news." She couldn't help but fib slightly; if she didn't, her mother would press for answers she didn't want to give.

"I appreciate your helping Katherine during this

difficult time." Her mother flashed her practiced corporate-wife smile. "I need to call the mortuary... and the medical examiner's office to see when they will release the body. If you'd excuse me," she said, looking to Troy and giving him an aloof nod before she made her way back to her cell phone in the living room.

"I'm so sorry about her. She can be insufferable at the best of times, and I swear, when she's stressed out, it gets a million times worse."

"Don't worry. She just lost her husband to violence. She has a right to be upset, even insufferable."

He took her hand and led her out of the dining room and into the kitchen, closing the door behind them. There was the ting of the doorbell and her mother's voice as more flowers were delivered. This was going to go on all day, this seesaw between incessant action and torturous malaise. Kate needed quiet. She needed to be alone. She needed to process all this. Instead, she was a slave to her mother's wishes.

"What happened to your dad?" Troy asked. "I want to help you get through this. I do. But I have to understand what exactly is going on before I can. What have you learned?"

Just the thought of what had happened to her father made a cold sweat rise on her skin. He didn't deserve to die the way he had, and though she knew she needed to tell Troy what had happened, she couldn't find the words. He'd let her remain silent on the ride here, not asking questions. She hadn't been able to manage a word or she would have sobbed uncontrollably. She barely had a grip.

"Take your time. I'm not going anywhere." Troy wrapped his arm around her shoulders, pulling her nearer to him.

She loved the feel of him against her, and the warmth that radiated from him. Just his touch helped her relax and feel ready to open up, not that talking about the attack was ever going to be easy. She was still coming to terms with what her mother had told her had happened. "We don't know everything yet, but according to Mom, he was found in his office this morning at 7:00 a.m. He had been shot once in the head and twice in the chest, and the initial responders noted stippling consistent with the shooter standing at a close range to the victim when they fired the gun." She swallowed and blinked fast, getting her emotions under control.

"So, then we know for sure that there was no sniper involved?" Troy asked. "It was up close and personal."

"The windows' glass was intact, so there is definitely nothing that came from outside his office. I got this from the officers on scene. The ones who called." Thinking about the logistics made some of the other things she was feeling dissipate. Maybe that was the best way to handle this. Keep emotions out of the way, be linear, be logical, and she would get through this. Better yet, they could find whoever it was who was responsible for her father's death. As for what would come of the killer after she found them, only time would tell.

"Do you know who is handling the investigation?" Troy asked.

"Due to the fact that he's my father, the FBI has offered to devote resources to the local law enforcement's investigation. So far, they haven't taken them up on the offer. I don't know why, but I'm sure the detectives will work their tails off to get to the bottom of this." She'd push on the FBI help if need be, but she didn't want to muddy the waters for the officers handling it right now. She knew local law could get their hackles raised if higher-ups got involved. It just slowed everything down.

Troy nodded. "Whatever you need from STEALTH, you got it. And Zoey can work on it from our tech angles. We can see what she can pull."

As she thought about Troy's offer, she realized all of the sacrifices he must've been making for her; sacrifices she hadn't totally thought about, until now. "I know you have a job to do, Troy. You don't have to stand beside me through all of this. If you need to go and do your job, that should come first." And his job had been investigating things at her father's company, so it might lead to his killer as well.

He squeezed her tighter, and, reaching up with his other hand, he caressed her cheek with his thumb. The simple action was unexpectedly sensual, and it made her weaken beneath him. Being touched like that by him made her realize how long it had been since someone had truly wanted to touch her.

"Babe, your father paid me to do a job. As far as I'm concerned, this all falls under that umbrella. If anything, I feel like…" He paused and his arm dropped from her. "Well, this all could be my fault. Maybe I was so focused on keeping you safe, when I should have been thinking about the bigger picture. I should've sent Mike over to watch your family."

She shook her head, vehemently. "This isn't your fault. How could you possibly know that there was somebody out there who wanted to hurt my father?"

"I had a feeling that this thing with the sniper wasn't over. I should have listened to my gut. Well, I guess I did… I knew something was wrong. That was how I found myself at your doorstep. But I think my entire focus was *off*. I let my personal feelings for you—and, yes, I admit it, I have feelings where you are concerned—cloud my perspective, and it may well have ended up costing your father his life."

She could hear the pain and anger and rage in his words, all of which were too big for what had happened to him in the situation. He must have been thinking about his ex, Tiffany, the one who had been killed by the EFP.

He was hurting just as she was. And though time was supposed to heal, she held no doubts that in this case all time was doing was making his pain more acute.

"There's plenty of security at the ConFlux building. My father had a well-trained security team watching out for him. Again, this isn't on you. My dad must've gotten into something he shouldn't have." Her chest threatened to collapse in on itself as she heard the truth of her words. "If anyone is to blame here, it's me. I actually listened to my dad and slow-walked the sniper case. I mean, I wasn't pushing hard on it like I usually do. I allowed him to affect my work. I screwed up. He ended up dead."

Troy sighed. "None of our hands are clean. All we can do now is to stop this from happening again. Only the murderer—and the person, people or group behind them—has any idea who else they are going to kill."

Chapter Twelve

Troy made his way out to his car and got inside. As soon as the door clicked shut, he dialed Zoey.

It didn't even have time to ring. "I heard about Solomon." Zoey sounded breathless. "I haven't managed to pull a lot of details—they're not releasing much to the public yet—but I'm sure you're thinking the same thing I am."

Troy gripped the steering wheel and put his head down against the cool leather. He gazed toward the colonial-style home that belonged to Kate's family. She was still inside, talking to her mother, no doubt bickering about some sort of family matter. It was no wonder Kate had become the strong woman she was after having to grow up with a mother who, though well raised and well-heeled, had the tongue of a cobra. Even making allowances for her grief, the woman was singularly unpleasant. "And what exactly is that?"

"I think you walked into a snake pit."

He opened his mouth to speak, but stopped. There

was no humanly way possible that Zoey could have known what he had been thinking, and yet the co-incidence was unsettling. "More than you know."

"Did you have time to get anywhere with the list of names I got you?" she asked, pushing forward without waiting for him to respond.

"Not yet."

"I can't blame you. Sounds like you have your hands full. Want me to pull some other members of your team in on this, give you some time to handle things with Kate?" Zoey asked, but he was aware that what she was really doing was trying to elicit a response that would tell her where his and Kate's relationship was currently standing.

"There's nothing beyond friendship between us."

"That's not what I said," Zoey countered.

"Yeah, but you and I both know what you meant. If you want to know if we've slept together, we haven't. We won't. We both have jobs to do."

Zoey laughed. "So, you have thought about it. Roger that."

He could feel the warmth rise in his cheeks. He didn't enjoy the sensation. "Why are you breaking my balls about this? About her? Right now, let's just focus on our next step. I don't need you stirring the pot."

Zoey laughed again, the sound full of mirth. "Got it. You're right," she said.

"I don't think I'll need any more team members. Mike is still working on this, right?"

"Yes, but I can call in your sister. She would be happy to come in and assist."

"Elle? Do you think bringing in K-9s would really be beneficial?"

"They are trained to track. Maybe they can pull something that the local LEOs are missing. A scent from the sniper, Solomon's shooter."

She had to have known she was grasping for straws on that one.

"No," Troy said, shaking his head though he was alone. He gripped the wheel tighter as he stared at the vehicle's make emblazoned on the steering wheel. "Why don't you see if you can get into the ConFlux security cameras and try to find who all came and went from the building in the last twenty-four hours before Solomon was found."

"You can't expect that I haven't already tried. Right now, I'm hitting brick walls," Zoey grumbled. "Well, figurative ones, at least. These guys, they had tight physical and cyber security. Which is good. The head of their IT department, Alexi Siegal, must have thought we were going to get attacked from all fronts."

That made it sound like his job in getting into the facility and finding weak spots was going to get a whole hell of a lot harder. If Zoey couldn't get in, he doubted he would be able to.

Maybe that was why there had been a sniper on the roof—as an even more extreme level of security. What if it had been part of Solomon's plan? Had he set them up to get shot at? No. He wouldn't do that. Not in front of the office where his own daughter worked. Right?

He wished he had a few answers instead of all these damn questions.

There was a tap on the passenger's-side window. "Got to go," he said to Zoey. He clicked the phone off in true Zoey Martin style.

Kate was standing there, so he unlocked the door and she got in. "I can't stand another minute in that house with my mother. It's hard enough dealing with Dad's death. Do you know she fired her maid and her gardener today? I'm not kidding—she is too much. This may actually have tipped her over the edge."

He wouldn't have blamed the woman if it had. "Does Deborah have someone she can talk to, a therapist or something?"

"I am sure she does, but if she doesn't, she definitely has access to just about anyone she would want to get." She rubbed her fingers together as she rolled her eyes.

"Do you hate your parents because they are affluent?" he asked, but as he spoke, he realized his mistake. "I'm sorry. I shouldn't ask something like that about your parents, at least not today."

"No, don't filter yourself. Ask me anything. I'll answer. Justice for my father comes first."

"I know this is a strange ask, but do you think you could get me and Zoey into ConFlux?"

"Probably. But why do you want in there—didn't

my father give you access when he hired STEALTH?" She paused.

"They wanted to see if we could hack into the system, not for us to sign on." He chuckled.

She nodded. "Unfortunately, I don't think I'm gonna be able to get you into my father's office, not with the investigation in full swing."

He reached over and took her hand, giving it a squeeze. "We have a lead on the sniper's possible identity. Though the sniper might not be related to your father's death, if I can get into the building, then maybe I can look a little bit deeper. I just need to poke around a bit."

Kate lifted their entwined hands and pressed her lips to the back of his, giving him a light kiss. "Whatever you need, it's yours."

He was sure she didn't mean it to sound as torrid as it had, but he still found himself getting aroused. There were many things he would like to do to her, but none of those things were a good idea. And yet he couldn't stop his gaze from moving slightly lower than it should have. She did have a nice body. He would have loved to feel her nipple against his tongue. He felt himself grow stiffer.

He cleared his throat, in a feeble attempt to rid his body of the threatening sensation of lust. This wasn't the right time. Her father had just died, and he needed to focus on finding the man's killer and comforting his daughter. He started the car and began driving toward downtown Missoula.

When they arrived, they encountered an entire squadron of patrol cars. The vehicles were congregated around the ConFlux building, a black coroner's van among them. It was backed in to a spot out front, its back tires on the sidewalk, as if it just waited to be filled.

He made sure to park away from too many prying eyes, but close enough that they could make a quick exit if they needed.

Though he knew he had to let go of Kate's hand, he hated it. Out there on the street, with all the police officers running around, they couldn't risk being seen as anything other than work colleagues. When he moved his hand from hers, her face said it all. She was crestfallen. He mouthed *I'm sorry*, but as he did, she looked away.

As they made their way toward the front doors, they opened. Four men walked through them, carrying a black body bag. "Stop," he said, taking Kate's arm and turning her away from the sight.

Something like that, watching her father loaded into the coroner's van, was likely to haunt her for the rest of her life. She didn't need this kind of trauma, not today or ever. Her job would bring her enough; she didn't need it in her personal life as well.

"Troy," she said, looking into his eyes. "It's okay. I'm going to be okay. You have to remember, I'm not like others. I've been trained to handle situations like these, to dissociate and embrace the suck sometimes."

"Just because you have the ability doesn't mean that your body always listens." He knew.

"I know you are trying to protect me, babe. But this isn't something you are going to be able to keep from hurting me. This is all painful—it's going to be no matter what you do or don't do. All I need you to do is stand by my side, help me get through these days and work with me to find and bring down whoever pulled the trigger."

He wanted to hold her and tell her that whatever she asked of him, he would deliver. Instead, he merely nodded.

She led the way to the entrance, watching as the men latched the van's doors closed and the driver sat down behind the wheel. The driver was talking to an officer as Troy and Kate walked into the office building through the vast marble-laced lobby, complete with a Greco-style water fountain at its heart. People Troy assumed were staffers were intermingled with police officers, asking and answering questions. No one seemed to notice them as they walked by the gurgling fountain and toward the metal detectors that led to the interior of the building.

There was a large desk in the reception area, and behind it were a man and a woman who looked as though they were the receptionists. The man looked up from his computer screen as they approached. The phone started to ring, and the woman beside him answered.

"Good morning. How can I help you?" he asked,

cutting them off from making their way over to the metal detectors and bypassing the checkpoint.

"Hi, I'm Kate Scot, Solomon's daughter."

The man blanched. "Oh, oh… Ms. Scot, I'm so very sorry to hear about your father. We've all been so upset after we learned what happened. They just…" He motioned after the van as it pulled away.

To think, her mother had already been pressing the issue about getting the medical examiner to release the body when they hadn't even gotten to see the man yet. Deborah was going to be in for a long emotionally rutted road.

"Do you mind if we go up?"

"It's… He's… You can, but…" The man stammered, clearly trying to come up with what he should or shouldn't do. But having no frame of reference, he finally sighed. "There are officers still doing their work in your father's office, but I'm sure there is probably someone up there you can speak to… someone who can help you."

"How about the ConFlux employees? Is everyone still on the clock, or did they all get sent home?"

"Um, they sent all nonessential personnel home today." He pressed a button. "You can step on through the detectors."

Kate shook her head. She reached down, took hold of her lanyard and pulled her badge from beneath her shirt, showing the man. "If you don't mind, we'll go around."

The man's face went impossibly paler. It was a

wonder the man was still able to form words. The receptionist nodded, hitting another button that opened the gate to the left of the metal detector.

Or maybe he isn't able to form words after all.

He could hardly blame the man; there were times when Kate had exactly the same effect on him; though, for entirely different reasons.

Kate's loafers clicked on the floor as she led them around security and they made their way to the elevator. They rode it up to the top, neither speaking for the short trip. The doors opened with a ping.

Standing in the hallway of the fourth floor was a group of city police officers. One of the men, wearing a suit, looked over at them. He sent Kate an apologetic stare as he meandered his way over toward them.

"If you don't mind, I'm going to take a peek around while you talk to this guy. Cool?" Troy asked.

She nodded, and under her breath, she said, "The detective is a friend of mine, but he's a talker. Take your time. I'll get more details about the murder."

Troy hurried away, walking down the hall in the opposite direction of the pack of officers and the detective and moving toward the restroom sign. Behind him, Kate was greeting her friend. Troy would have preferred to have had Kate with him so she could tell him about the different offices and their purposes, but on the other hand, the freedom allowed him to poke around on his own.

He slipped into the first empty office he came to

on his right, checking over his shoulder and making sure that no one was paying him any mind. He closed the door behind himself.

The room was small, cramped and full of paperwork. It looked like the kind of office that belonged to an intern, some poor unpaid schlep who was at the bottom of the proverbial hill. When he'd started out in contracting, he had been the poor schlep... the guy who had to take the nighttime runs, when the chances of taking a bullet were even higher than they were during the day.

He had been forced to earn his place on every one of the teams he'd ever been a part of. But when it came to him and Kate, they were just an instant team fueled by a common goal and mutual anger.

He flipped through a few of the papers, but most looked like they were interoffice memos, and the only thing that struck him as odd was that a company like ConFlux would still use such an antiquated system for informing their employees about upcoming events. Maybe it was just that some old habits died hard...or, like in many branches of the federal government, the best kinds of security were the ones that couldn't be hacked. But, in situations like these, where security was stretched thin due to the unusual events, what couldn't be hacked could definitely be stolen.

He glanced around the room; there wasn't a camera in sight. Taking out his phone, he dialed Zoey.

She answered even though he hadn't heard it ring. "Did you get in to ConFlux?"

"Yep, I'm in an intern's office now."

"Is there a computer available?" Zoey asked, a falsetto to her voice he didn't think he'd heard from her before.

He walked to the other side of the desk and sat down in the cheap, squeaky rolling chair. He clicked on the screen. "I'm there."

"Great. Let's hope we have a Bob here."

"What in the hell is a Bob?"

"In every work environment, there is always that one employee, 'Bob,' who is a bit unaware when it comes to the importance of security, especially cybersecurity—maybe it's with their personal information or the company's. Doesn't matter. This person is the one who clicks on the phishing email and lets in the hackers. All we need is to find the Bob and we can crack the company."

He still wasn't sure he totally understood what she meant, but as he looked around the cluttered room, if there was a "Bob," Troy was probably in his office. Sometimes it paid to be lucky. Though, they didn't put CEOs' offices between a bathroom and an elevator.

The computer was typical, the usual PC that could be found in just about any office. There was a flashing cursor on the screen, waiting for him to input the key code in order to get to the home screen. "Zoey, I have a problem. Need a PIN. Any ideas?"

"Whose office are you in?"

He hadn't seen a name on the door and there were a variety of names all over the memos he had flipped through. Glancing at the walls, he saw there was a picture of a young family, a husband with a wife who was holding an infant. "Whoever this office belongs to, they likely just had a baby."

"Good," Zoey said. He could hear the click of keys in the background. "Anything else that can help pin this person down?"

Beside the computer screen was a mug. It read Daryl.

"I think his first name is Daryl." He chuckled. That was one name that was entirely too close to Bob.

There was a burst of keystrokes. "Got it," Zoey said. She paused for a few seconds. "Try 0127."

He typed in the pin number and he was met with the home screen. "Holy crap, Zoey. That worked. How in the hell did you know that?"

"I could lie and play it cool by telling you it was a lucky guess, or I'm that good, but that's hardly it… That is the birthday of his son."

She was damn good at her job. It was no wonder that she and her family had started their own contracting company, one with deep ties throughout the US and several foreign governments.

"Now, I want you to go into his email. Give me his address."

He clicked on a few keys, taking him to the man's

inbox, and he read off the email address associated with the account.

"Good," Zoey said, typing. "In a few minutes, I'm going to send an email. It will have the subject line *Bagels for today's meeting*. Click on it. Download. And I will handle the rest." The phone line went dead.

That was one thing he was never going to get used to with Zoey, no matter how many times he was on the receiving end, and as unsettling as her hanging up was, he found he liked it. No fluff.

He filtered through some of the other emails on the man's computer, but most appeared to be as unimportant as the memos he had first seen. The only one that looked at all interesting was from a woman at the company. Mr. New Baby must have been unsatisfied at home.

His dislike for the intern grew, and the tiny ping of guilt for hijacking the man's computer he had felt deep—make that *very* deep—in his core disappeared. If anyone found out the company had been hacked, they might eventually find out whose computer and account had been the weak link and the man would be fired.

At least, here was hoping.

A new email pinged—bagels. He clicked on it and did as Zoey had instructed. He half expected the computer to flicker as he downloaded her file, but nothing happened aside from a pop-up that announced that his document had been successfully downloaded.

No wonder there was a Bob problem; it was entirely too easy for someone who wasn't aware of danger to download malicious code or malware. This, this right here was the reason banks and insurance companies were forced to pay billions in IT security each and every year.

There was a knock on the door and he flipped off the computer. Job done. This was in Zoey's hands now.

He cleared his throat. "Yeah?"

"You in there?" Kate asked. "Can I come in?"

He stood up and walked over to the door, opening it. She was standing with the detective, and from the look on her face, she was deeply uncomfortable. The man must have been asking questions.

"Thank you for letting me get into my office. I just needed to get a couple files sent out to clients today. You know, no rest for the weary," he said, careful to cover up any kind of tells that would give away his lie. "Besides, I know Mr. Scot wouldn't have wanted work to come to a halt—and deadlines missed—all because of him. He was a good man." He gave a respectful nod of the head, hoping that the detective would buy it.

He walked out of the office, carefully closing the door behind him as he looked up. The detective was giving him a once-over, analyzing his body language. Thankfully, the detective didn't know he was sizing up a man who had spent his entire life learning how to avoid detection, and when detected, learning how to get out of trouble.

"If our department was as dedicated as you, we would always stop crimes before they were even committed. Good friend you got there, Agent Scot." He gave Kate a pat to the shoulder, solidifying the physical bond as well as trying to reassure her. "I got to get back in there, but I hope you know...you need anything, got any more questions... I'll give you what I can."

Kate nodded and smiled at the detective, but Troy could sense the fire behind her smile. It made him wonder if the detective could as well.

"I'll walk you guys out," the detective said, making it clear that they were no longer welcome.

Chapter Thirteen

Fury flooded Kate as Troy drove her to her home. She hadn't been this angry since she had gotten a flat tire on the way to her final interview for the FBI.

She had thought the sacrifices had been worth it right up until now. How dare a detective think he could pull rank on her and force her out of an investigation that involved her family? Sure, she didn't have jurisdiction, but there was a damn thing called professional courtesy.

He should have thrown her a solid, just as she had done by not involving the FBI from the get-go. The last time they had worked together, she had broken a murder case for him, pulling strings in order to get him DNA samples in record time so that he could file official charges before the suspect disappeared. While he had thanked her, he had never repaid her.

That was the last time she helped him out.

She sighed.

That wasn't true. She allowed herself to be furious, but in her heart of hearts, she knew that if he came to her with another case that she could help in bringing down a bad guy, she wouldn't pass up the chance. She loved to make the guilty pay. It was what kept her going.

Troy parked his car in front of her house, not hiding. There was nothing wrong with her having a male colleague over during the day. And if someone wanted to judge, let them judge lest they be judged. She was over it.

"You know you don't have to talk to me. I can tell you are upset. I just hope you aren't upset with me. I was trying to make the best of a bad situation back there, and—"

She glanced over at him, shocked. "What? You think I'm mad at you?"

"I should have been in and out of that office before your detective friend even noticed. I compromised you. That wasn't my intention. I was just working on the fly." As he spoke, his words came faster and faster as his anxiety seemed to rise.

Kate softened as he tried to recover from his perceived misstep, one that she hadn't even noticed. He was so adorable flustered.

"I'm not mad about anything you did. Actually, the detective didn't even notice, and even when I went to get you, he didn't seem to think anything. You played that off perfectly. I was impressed."

He gave her a confused look. "So, why are you so upset?"

She rolled her neck, dispelling some of the stress

at the admission she was going to have to make. "I was annoyed that we were dismissed. I didn't manage to pull anything about what happened to my father. They wouldn't let me into his office, or even close enough to catch a glimpse of the crime scene..." She paused. "Why?"

Troy shrugged. "I think there are a lot of odd things happening... Too many for them to be just random."

She was more than aware of that fact. "Who are the people on Zoey's list—the sniper suspects?"

"One's a guy named Sal Baker, then one Chris Michaels, and the other is...*stupid*. I told her that she couldn't have been right." He waved off his avoidance of telling her the other name like it was of no concern.

"You can't do that to me," Kate argued. "Either tell me the whole truth or nothing." Her voice was shriller than she had intended, but she didn't apologize. Not today, not with everything spiraling the drain. "Same team."

He frowned. "You... I—I'm sorry. I'm not trying to upset you. It's not like that. I'm all about us working efficiently together. I just don't think Agent Peahen would ever do anything as stupid as taking potshots off a building at private contractors or you. He's not the type."

"Are you kidding me?" She shook her head slightly, like the little motion would help her to make sense of what he had said. If only it would have worked.

"I told you…" Troy said, shrugging.

Peahen? Peahen a sniper? No.

There was no damn way. He was capable of many things. And he was definitely the kind of man who wouldn't have qualms about acting all tough, but he was not the kind who would pull the trigger when it wasn't in the line of duty.

"Yeah, you're right. He's not our guy." She chuckled at the craziness of the idea. "Besides, he said he's been in Salt Lake City."

"At the time of the shooting?"

"I don't know." She was suddenly exhausted. "When Peahen showed up on my doorstep the other night, he just said he had been passing through from SLC. I assumed he had been down there doing something with the regional headquarters. I doubt he would try to kill somebody and then turn around and head out to see me."

"You're preaching to the choir."

"And, plus… He has no motivation," she continued, trying to convince herself that she had to be right.

"Again…" Troy said, as he stepped out of the car and walked around, opening her door for her. He held out his hand for her to take as she stepped out. "I think we should look deeper into the Sal guy. See what kind of motivation he would have for taking out the surveillance team hired to look into the company. You don't know him, do you?"

"Sal?" she asked, grabbing her keys out of her purse as they walked up to the front door, and she let them in. "I only know the higher-ups from the company, the kinds my father would take out on golf trips around the country when they tried to work government officials in order to get new and greater manufacturing contracts."

"Sal wasn't one of them?"

She shrugged. "I don't think so. I am only invited to the holiday parties and a few of the bigger luncheons when he wants—wanted—to show me off like a prize pony to his cronies." The door clicked shut as they made their way inside.

She put her purse on the table next to the door, slipped off her suit jacket and hung it on the closet's doorknob. There was a little dribble of coffee just above her left breast that she hadn't noticed before. She would have to change before they went back out. "If Sal is in the upper crust, then he was new to the organization."

"Yes. Finally." Troy sounded excited as he walked and sat down in the chair in front of the television. He took out his phone and started pressing buttons.

"What are you so excited about?"

"He's new. He has a weapon like the one the sniper used. Maybe he got himself hired at the company just to do some damage or spying. The Russians love that approach." Troy smiled.

"Don't you think that is a little too Cold War style?" she asked.

"You can't tell me that it's not a valid possibility. These kinds of companies have information leaks all the time. It's why I have a job. And…more often than not, there is a foreign government behind the infiltration—be it in person or through technology. Thinking about technology…" He sent her a sly smile.

"You gonna tap Sal's phone lines? See if you can catch him speaking Russian?" she asked with a sarcastic laugh.

"Hey, don't judge. Your friends in the CIA used to do that kind of thing all the time… Though, admittedly, the tech has gotten a bit better since the 1980s. I don't think they try to tap as many landlines these days."

"Which makes them just about safer than any form of technology," she countered. "At least with phone lines only the person tapping in can hear what is being said. With cell phones…the possibilities of seeing, reading, hearing and looking into search histories are nearly endless."

He laughed. "If I look around, am I also going to find a telegraph? A dictionary for Morse code?"

"Don't judge," she echoed, feeling a little bit embarrassed. "There is nothing wrong with knowing an antiquated form of communication like Morse code. You never quite know when something like that can come in handy."

"Do you actually know Morse code?" He gave her a skeptical look.

"I do." She couldn't help the pride that flickered through her voice.

"Me too," he said, laughing. "I thought I was the

only nerd out there who loved that kind of thing. In my free time, which I admit I haven't had a whole lot of lately, I also used to love to do origami. I did it with my mom before she died. It was kind of our thing. I haven't made anything since the day she died."

"Oh my goodness, that is so sweet. What was your favorite thing to make?"

"I always liked the cranes," he said, a nostalgic smile on his lips. "She would tell me a story about how they were the symbol for hope, happiness and healing. And if a person folded one thousand cranes, whatever he wished for most would come true."

"What would you wish for, right now?" For a split second, she hoped he would tell her that what he most wished for was her, but then she brushed away the naive hope.

There was a heavy silence as he pursed his lips. Finally, he stood up.

Is he going to walk over to me? she thought.

Her heart slammed against her ribs and her palms instantly started to sweat as he drew nearer. Yet, instead of stepping in front of her, he walked past her and toward the kitchen. The only things he left for her were the thin scent of his cologne and the cool breeze in his wake.

She was so stupid. Hope had a hell of a way of jabbing a person in the gut.

From the kitchen, she could make out the sounds of him opening a cupboard, then the running of the faucet. He came back bearing two glasses of water.

"Here." He offered her a glass, and as she took it, she was careful to avoid his fingers.

If she touched him, she would lose what little control she had over her emotions—the least favorite of them being rejection. She was already on a razor's edge after her father's death, then being pushed out of the investigation.

She should have never let her guard down when it came to him. In her current state, she saw heartache around every corner, and she set herself up for it by being way too needy right now.

They were nowhere near a relationship. They'd been thrown together on this case, and one thing after another had led to heightened emotions.

Though she had promised him that he could trust her, she had never made him promise the same when it came to her.

Then again, she was being silly. They were just feeling each other out before becoming overly invested. If anything, it was good that he had rebuffed her coy advance now. In the end, it was going to save her heartache.

And who had time for a relationship anyway?

She certainly didn't. Not with her father's death. Not with the investigation. Not with her sister coming into town and all the things that would happen as soon as the medical examiner released her father's body to the family. Her mom could really use her help handling all the details, even if her mother acted like an unstoppable and unwavering freight train.

All of that activity was going to catch up with her eventually, and when it did, she was going to come to the end of her tracks, teeter over the edge of exhaustion and fall into the canyon of grief.

Kate drained the glass of water in one long swig, careful not to catch Troy's gaze as he stood beside her. As she finished, he held out his hand, motioning to take her empty glass.

"Thanks," she said, handing it over.

"Do you need some more? Hungry?"

She hadn't eaten yet today, but food was the last thing on her mind. Even if there had been a full spread sitting in front of her, she wasn't sure she would have eaten a single bite. "Unless you have a bucket of Red Vines, I'm good." She tried to smile, but it felt stale and flat.

"I can whip you up some eggs at the very least, if you'd like." He motioned toward the kitchen.

"Nah. Really, I'm okay."

"You sure? All of a sudden, you seem *off*. Are you tired?"

She nodded. Yes, she was tired. And confused. And wanting something from him she wasn't sure he was offering. "So, what do you have on Chris and Sal? Anything?"

He took a drink of water and set the glasses down on the coffee table. "Is it okay if I put these here?" he asked, motioning toward them.

"I'm not my mother. My house is furnished by

IKEA, not an interior decorator. My most expensive piece probably cost like twenty bucks," she said.

"Yeah, right. This place is great." Unexpectedly, he walked over to her and took both of her hands. He looked her in the eyes. "I know what you are doing—I know you are trying to be cool. I know what you were hoping I would say about my wish. I didn't mean to hurt you."

Though she could hear his words and they were making their way into her logical brain, all they did was make the pain and embarrassment she was feeling worse. "I don't know what you mean," she said, scrunching her face in forced denial.

"You can lie to a lot of people and probably get away with it, but that will never be the way it is with me. I've been trained to read this kind of thing, remember?" He let go of her left hand as he reached up and cupped her face.

She nodded, but resisted the urge to lean into his touch even though he was being sweet and sensitive—exactly the kind of man she fantasized about.

"I have an idea of what you are going through right now. And though you are handling it all with a level of strength, grace and aplomb that even the royals would be envious of, you are hurting. I can see it on you."

Her chest tightened and tears started to well in her eyes. No. He couldn't bring her to her knees like this—she was stronger than this—he couldn't see her cry.

"It's okay to feel, Kate. You're home. You are safe

with me. You can be your real self. You don't have to put on a front for me. I am not going to judge you for processing what you are going through—it's not healthy to push that crap down and not deal with it. I know." He ran his thumb over her cheek. "Let out your grief. Let's get through this together. I'm your friend. Whatever you say, whatever you need, I'm yours to open up to."

If only he had stopped at *I'm yours*.

A lump rose in her throat and she tried to swallow it back, but it was futile. He leaned in, pressing his forehead to hers as he put his other hand to her face. "Kate, it's okay to cry."

Though she hadn't given it permission, a single tear slipped down her cheek. Maybe it was his kindness, his sweetness or his strength in his candor, but whatever it was, it tore down the barrier of her heart.

Tears flooded her cheeks.

Her father was dead. Her mother was a mess. A fellow agent was possibly on the take. And they were no closer to solving any of it than they were when she had first received the news of the murder.

Murder. The word reverberated through her. Though she had heard it spoken and had spoken of it often, it was as if she was hearing it for the first time. This time the word was *hers*—it was like a pebble being thrown in the lake of her world. There would be ripples of what had happened today throughout every day for the rest of her life.

The only thing she could do to reduce their frequency was to do as Troy said…and to find justice.

At least she wasn't going through this completely alone or with her mother. In the state her family was currently in, she would have to be cool and collected. There was no room for real emotions, only actions.

Troy brushed the tears from her cheeks as others followed quickly behind. Letting go of her face, he wrapped her in his arms and pulled her close. Her sobs rattled against him, but instead of loosening his grip, he held her only tighter like he was her anchor in this tempest.

She loved him.

As she cried, she thought of Neruda, Sonnet XVII:

I love you as certain dark things are to be loved,

in secret, between the shadow and the soul…

I love you without knowing how, or when, or from where.

I love you straightforwardly, without complexities or pride;

so I love you because I know no other way than this…

Though she was feeling as low as she ever had, the high of the possibility of someday loving him openly—even as only a dear friend—helped to calm the storm inside of her.

"You are going to get through this. We can do it together," he whispered into her hair.

She nodded, sniffing as she tried to keep from getting his shirt more wet than absolutely necessary from her tears. The man didn't deserve to become her tissue.

"Thank you, Troy." She laid her head against his chest and listened to the beat of his heart. The sound worked as a calming drum, stanching her tears.

She would grieve. But today, she wouldn't have to go through this pain alone; she had love.

Chapter Fourteen

The last woman he had held while crying had been Elle when they had lost their parents. Ever since then, even when breaking up with the few girlfriends he'd had, he had made it out of there before the tears had started to fall. Tears were his weakness, far too *feely*. At least they had been, until now.

He brushed her hair back from her face and rubbed her back. She didn't seem like the type of woman who cried easily, especially around other people, and yet here she was, sobbing her heart out to him. She could open up, be free to express herself, and he was actually glad to be the one holding her while she let go.

Did that mean this was love?

Was what he was feeling something more than it should be? Or was this feeling inside of him toward her exactly right?

He couldn't deny the fact that he wanted more. That he wanted all of her. To see her wake up in the morning. To sit with her while her hair was all messy and she sipped on her first cup of coffee. He would love to have her cold feet press against him in bed at night. And he wanted to know her favorite foods. Her favorite songs. He wanted to know everything about her.

Maybe he was sick or possibly losing his mind. He wasn't like this when it came to the opposite sex. Sure, he liked women. And he liked naked women. And he liked naked women who liked him. But he had always been careful to keep the naked women away from his naked feelings.

And now here she was, fully clothed and edging into the feelings he so carefully tried to conceal. Odd as it was, he felt more naked than if he had been standing there unclothed.

If he opened up to her right now, while they were both emotionally compromised, it would be the equivalent of a drunken late-night phone call. Things would be said that couldn't be taken back in the morning, things that were probably best left for a time when they were both working from a place of fully available and uncompromised emotional facilities—that was, if they were going to be said at all.

She leaned back, and reaching up, she wiped the last bit of wetness from her cheeks with the sleeve of her white button-down shirt. "I'm sorry. I don't know why I…"

"You don't have anything to apologize for," he said, meaning every syllable.

They stood there in silence for a long moment,

and he thought about taking her face in his hands
and kissing those perfect pink lips. They were the
color of Starburst candies and they probably tasted
just as sweet.

Late-night phone call.

The words rang in his mind.

Her stomach grumbled. She had told him that she
wasn't hungry, unless he had Red Vines—he was
more of a Twizzlers man himself.

"Babe, you need to eat something." He hurried
into the kitchen and opened up her fridge before she
had the chance to argue. She could say she wasn't
hungry all she wanted, but her body told him the
truth.

There was a small rectangle of cheese, a pint of
milk, a carton of eggs, ketchup and mustard and a
bunch of bananas. There was the scrape of a chair
as she sat down at the bar.

"Seriously, who puts bananas in the fridge?" He
laughed, breaking one off and handing it to her before turning back and grabbing the eggs, milk and
cheese.

"You are lucky I have anything in there. I'm not
much of a chef. But, if you look in the freezer, there
are some frozen single-serving pizzas. We could
throw a couple of them in the microwave."

He laughed. "I'm here. I'm going to take care of
you. And, as luck has it, I'm actually a pretty good
chef—not that you have much to work with here,

but I bet I can whip us up a mean set of scrambled eggs and toast."

"No soufflés?" she teased, but there was still the rasp of post-cry pulling at her voice.

"Beggars can't be choosers, pumpkin."

She gave a little laugh. "Why do I get the feeling that you calling me *pumpkin* is just about as close to a declarative statement as I'm ever going to get from you?"

"What do you mean *declarative statement*?" he asked, grabbing a bowl and cracking an egg into it.

"You know… That you *like* me." She smiled.

Her eyes were red and puffy from her crying, but the softness from her voice mixed with her sweet grin made her seem even more beautiful than he had realized before. She was remarkably breathtaking in all of her imperfection.

"Do you want me to *like* you?" he asked, suddenly feeling entirely too much like a high schooler than an adult man.

She wrung her hands, playing the high school love interest almost perfectly. She shrugged, the motion weighted with so much meaning that he couldn't figure her out. "It's been a while since I've had a man around my house," she said, looking up at him like she was afraid that he would mind that she had a life before him. "My ex… He took my dog when he moved out. And seriously, I can't go through losing another dog. It broke my heart."

"You only miss the dog?" He smirked. "And you don't have a dog now, right? For me to steal?"

She sent him a look of surprise, then a guilty smile. "Why would I miss a man who treated me like crap? The dog loved me unconditionally. If anything, the only thing I felt guilty about was that I didn't fight harder to keep Max. My ex was good to him, but there's no way he could have loved Max as much as I did—the only thing he loved was himself."

"Ouch," Troy said, laughing. "I hate when you end a relationship and you don't stay friends. I know it's harder, but I always think that if you loved someone, you will love them forever—even if you find that they're not the right person for you. And, at the very least, they deserve your respect."

She cringed, her face pinching. "So, you're saying that you think less of me because I think my ex is a total jackass?"

He laughed. "I didn't say that I've remained friends with all my exes. I just said I don't like it when things turn sour. Sometimes there is just too much vitriol and hurt for two people to keep on liking each other. Though, even when I don't like someone, I *try*—and *try* is the key word—to be as close to respectful as I can be… But a man only has so much willpower."

She laughed. "So, you do have one or two who you can't stand?"

"I haven't dated a ton of women, and I would say that I would still help all of them if there was a subway train threatening to hit them...but there is a short list of exes whom I would wait until the last second to save."

"Ohhhh, ouch." She laughed, the sound from deep within her.

Just the sound made him lighten. Yes, he definitely loved this woman, but he couldn't face that. Not after Tiffany. Love led to pain.

He made quick work of the breakfast as she scrolled through her phone. "According to what I was able to pull, and from what my mother is saying, Sal Baker is one of my father's new hires. He came on as a new engineering director for our machining plant."

Before Solomon's murder, he'd chatted with Zoey, who had spent the night digging into the company's data. Though she hadn't found much yet, she had finally nailed down the man's identity.

"You didn't talk to your mother about someone we are investigating, did you?" he asked, stopping as he scooped the eggs onto her plate. The toast popped up, but he didn't move as he tried to make sense of what Kate had said.

"It's okay. My mom isn't the kind who would think anything of it. And besides, I asked her about all the people my father was working with." She waved him off, like he was making something out of nothing, but the misstep made his hackles rise.

Zoey would be irate if she thought he had compromised her investigation in any way.

"Kate," he said, taking the toast and slathering it with butter before handing it over to her. "I don't think you telling your mother anything, or even asking her any questions, is a good idea."

She popped a bit of egg into her mouth and slowly chewed, like she was carefully picking and choosing her answers before responding to him. "Troy, I appreciate your concern. You know I do. But just because I'm a woman doesn't mean that my training in the FBI has had no effect. I am a competent agent. I know how to get the information I need without anyone being the wiser."

"I wasn't questioning your training. I know you are amazing at what you do, but that doesn't mean that I am not going to worry about you—especially in a case like this. Sometimes, when things involve our family members, it is damn hard to remain objective. It's easy to be blind when it comes to those we love."

What was he blind about when it came to her?

He ate a piece of toast, watching her as she plowed through the plate of food that she had sworn she wasn't hungry for. With her plate empty, she sat back and yawned. He glanced outside, and for the first time, he noticed it had grown dark. Where had the day gone? It wasn't lost on him that when it came to spending time with Kate, time had a way of racing by—even when he had been outside and just standing guard.

"I know this is going to sound strange," Kate said,

wiping her mouth, "but…would you mind staying here tonight? I have a spare bedroom." She pointed down toward the stairs. "It's not a king-sized bed or anything, it's only a twin, but it's comfy. I—I just don't want to be alone tonight."

He didn't want to be alone either, but he wasn't thinking about the kind of alone that meant sleeping in separate beds… Then again, he didn't mean that he wanted sex either. What he really wanted, more than anything else, was intimacy and to hold her while she fell asleep.

If only she felt the same way about him.

But no, she wanted him to sleep in a separate bed. If nothing else, at least he would get to see her again in the morning…and he could be the man she needed.

"Babe, even if you wanted to have me sleep on the moon in order to keep you safe, I would do it for you." He took her plate, afraid that if he looked at her, he would see his words register and her response would make the threadbare leash he had on his feelings for her give way and he would run straight into her arms.

"Lucky for you, the guest bedroom isn't quite so far away." She stood up with the squeak of the chair and made her way around the kitchen island. She stepped behind him and put her arms around his waist. "Thank you, Grim. Thank you for everything you do for me."

The air left his lungs in a gush, the string that held his feelings in check. "You're welcome, Scythe."

SHE HAD SET everything out that he needed for a shower, and when he got out of the bathroom between their bedrooms, her door was closed and her light was off. He stood quietly in the hall and he was sure he could hear the soft sounds of her sleeping.

Kate was his angel. He would take a bullet for her, even if their friendship went nowhere beyond where they were.

After going to the guest bedroom, he lay there until a light, fitful sleep finally overtook him. It didn't feel like it had been very long when he was awakened by the creak of a door. He gripped the gun he had tucked under his pillow, but he was careful not to move and give his enemy any more of an advantage than they already had.

There was barely a sound, but he could pick up the rasp of footsteps on the carpet as someone approached the other side of the bed. He gripped the gun, readying to pull and shoot. No one was going to get the drop on him.

And then she sighed. The sound was soft and quiet, but it was as clear and filled with meaning as if Kate had shouted his name.

His grip loosened on his gun as he realized that, for now, they were safe from the outside world— from each other, well, that was an entirely different matter.

He had to pretend to be asleep; if she had wanted to wake him up, she would have. Perhaps what she needed right now was just the pacifying touch of someone who cared for her.

Whatever she needs...

She slipped between the sheets and, ever so gently, put her arm around him as she nestled into his body. Her breasts were pressed into his back, but he couldn't tell whether or not she was wearing any clothes, thanks to his shirt. No matter what, he didn't want to ruin the sensation by moving.

"I know you're awake," she whispered, as though the world would hear them.

He wasn't sure how to respond. He needed to say something, to acknowledge her, but he wasn't about to ask her what she wanted or needed from him. Instead, he gave a sleepy, soft grumble.

"I'm sorry. Go back to sleep. I didn't mean to wake you," she said, her voice louder and quicker than it had been before, as if she suddenly was embarrassed for coming to him in the night.

"No," he said, turning his head toward her. "Don't be sorry." He reached down and took her hand. He lifted her fingers to his mouth and gave them a kiss. "I'm glad you are here."

Her body relaxed. "I was cold."

Oddly enough, she didn't feel cool. Instead, she felt warmer than he did, but he wasn't about to argue the point. "Here," he said. Letting go of her hand, he rolled over. "Why don't I hold you until

Danica Winters 185

you get warmed up. I don't want my little scythe to be chilled."

He expected her to roll over and scoot her body into his so he could spoon her, wrapping her in the warmth of his core. And yet she stayed still, facing him.

"That's not quite how I wanted you to warm me up." There was a sultry lilt to her voice he hadn't heard her use before.

His body instantly reacted and he pressed against his boxers.

Though his brain screamed at him that this wasn't a good idea, that he should try to talk her down from this ledge—one that once they stepped over there was no coming back from—his body took over. There was only one thought... He loved her.

Kate lifted her chin, beckoning him to kiss her. Who was he to deny her?

As his lips touched hers, every feel-good chemical in his body swirled into his system, and he could sense himself grow high. He would have never thought just a kiss could be better than any sexual experience he'd ever had before.

Their kiss—it was like someone had opened up the floodgates after a spring thaw. Everything, every wintry pent-up emotion, laugh, cry and fear, came gushing out as her tongue caressed his bottom lip.

He reached up and pressed his hand into the center of her back, pulling her impossibly nearer to him. They couldn't be close enough. He wanted all of her.

Running his thumb over the subtle curve of her spine, he felt only the silky smoothness of her flesh. She had come to his bed naked.

Oh, for all that is good... I have to be dreaming.

If he was, he never wanted to wake up. This could be the moment that he could be stripped from the earth and he would die a happy and complete man.

She gently kissed him, loving him as he traced his fingers down her back, finding the thick round curves of her hips and her upper thigh. Nothing impeded his downward descent. He moved his fingers in small circles around the dimples of her ass, marking them in his mind as places his lips wished to travel.

Though Kate wasn't what media deemed perfect, she was better. She was imperfect, different in the way she viewed the world and people in it, and flawed in the sense that she was authentically herself.

And, truth be told, perfect was boring. Perfect was merely a mundane conglomeration of traits. Yes, perfection was striven for in most social circles, but it was also the prison that kept people from speaking from their hearts and finding the passion that came with being free.

Being with her was being free. Free to love. Free to explore. Free to experience everything he'd ever wanted to feel.

He stopped, letting his hand rest on her hip. As he stopped, she touched his chest right over his heart.

She didn't say anything as their kisses paused and their lips brushed against each other.

She sighed, the cool air an odd sensation against the warmth where their kisses had heated.

He yearned to tell her that he loved her, but that was the one part of him that was still so scarred. That was one way he would never be free. That word only brought death and pain. He couldn't do that to either one of them.

But he could give her his body and receive hers—and love her in a way that she needed.

He moved to his elbow, kissing her lips and then kissing every millimeter until he was between her thighs. Sensing the motions of her body, the sounds of her sighs and the tightening of her grip on his hair, he worked her.

"Troy," she cried out, calling his name like it was the elixir of life. She uttered guttural sounds as she pulsed beneath him, riding the pleasure he reveled in bringing her.

Her body quaked as he brought her to the precipice. Smiling, he kissed the creamy skin of her inner thighs and rested his head on her leg.

And just when he had thought he couldn't be more turned on or more satisfied, she looked down at him. She looked sleepy, her eyes the hazy squint of the well sated. "I… You…"

Her inability to form words made his smile widen. "Having a hard time speaking?" he teased.

She nodded with a dazed smile. "You think you can handle more?"

"I could be down here for hours, babe."

She laughed. "Again, that's not quite what I was thinking."

"Then what exactly did you have in mind?"

Kate reached down and pulled him up toward her, kissing the wetness from his lips. "This time, it's going to be all about you."

Chapter Fifteen

There were a variety of kinds of sex. There was the first time, second time, the millionth time. Then there was the kind that came with partners who were only passing in the night—the kind full of passion and laughter, the type that both sought to please the other, but also themselves. Last night, it had been all of it, all wrapped into one.

And Kate had never had better.

She moved around the kitchen, humming as she put together a batch of pancakes and fried them up on the griddle. The bacon, the stuff from the package she'd found deep in the recesses of her freezer, was crackling in the microwave.

It felt good to be cooking for a man again. It was odd to think that the last time she had actually *cooked* was before the breakup. But it wasn't the same when a person lived alone.

Troy came walking into the kitchen, rubbing the sleep from his eyes. He smiled as he saw her. "Good morning, beautiful. Something smells awesome."

"There's coffee in the pot," she said, motioning toward the appliance.

He grabbed a mug. "You want a refill?" he asked, grabbing the carafe.

"I already had two. Thanks, though." She hummed, smiling as she flipped the next pancake.

He took a long drink of his coffee, then stepped behind her and wrapped his arms around her waist. "Babe, thank you for last night. You are effing fantastic."

"I don't know why you would think you would need to thank me. You did most of the heavy lifting." She giggled as she sent him a coy glance over her shoulder.

He kissed her lips as she looked back.

In this stolen moment, she was completely, blithely satisfied. For once, she was *happy*.

She scooped a stack of pancakes onto his plate and motioned toward the microwave. "Grab a couple of strips." She handed him his plate. "Here, you," she said, giving him a kiss on his cheek.

"Babe, you're the best."

"I could say the same of you." In that simple moment and exchange, she had a feeling that this—this could be their future.

She wanted nothing more.

Grabbing a plate from the cupboard, she heard a crack to the right of her ear. Fire erupted from the side of her head. Instinctively, she reached up and touched the place near her earlobe that burned.

Bringing her fingers down, she saw they were covered in blood.

In what seemed like slow motion, she turned and spotted Troy lunging toward her as the flour she had set on the counter beside the griddle exploded. White powder filled the air. Troy's body connected with hers and his arms wrapped around her waist as they fell onto the floor together.

"Stay down!" he yelled, pulling a gun she hadn't realized he was carrying from the back of his pants as she lay there on the floor just watching.

Someone was shooting...*at her*. Why? From where? What in the hell was going on?

Troy moved behind the kitchen island in a squatting position facing the direction from where the bullet had come. Whoever was shooting must have been posted somewhere behind her house. There were several houses that were at the same or higher level than hers, so the shooter could have been anywhere.

She was going to need to invest in blackout blinds, something that no one could see through.

Be in the moment. She had to stay in the moment. She couldn't dissociate now.

She belly-crawled toward the living room, making sure that she stayed behind cover as she moved. Beside the doorway, by the pantry, was a Glock 43x she had bought and stashed for an occasion just like this one, one she'd never thought would actually happen.

Pulling it out, she made sure it was loaded. One hollow point in the chamber. It was a single-stack magazine; she had nine more hollow points, if need dictated. Hopefully, if she got her sights on the shooter, it would take only one.

But odds were good that whoever was shooting at her, they weren't doing it from right outside the window. This person, whoever it was, was probably perched somewhere high, waiting for the right moment to take another shot. This shooter was probably the same sniper who had left them high and dry, with only a few leads to use in order to discover their identity.

She had a sinking feeling that if they didn't get him this time, she would be living the rest of her life constantly looking over her shoulder. That was, if she lived past today.

There was another whiz and crack as the next round struck the pantry door, not six inches from her head.

"They are shooting from up high." She could hear the terror in her voice, but she tried to temper it as she called to Troy. "They're probably coming at us from the old manor. It's about a hundred yards out, at your one o'clock position. You see anybody?"

Troy moved slightly to his left, peering up over the counter but then just as quickly ducking down again. They didn't need the sniper taking any more potshots, and they definitely didn't need him getting lucky and actually hitting either one of them.

"We need a distraction. Something that is going to pull our shooter's attention while I can get closer.

Or else we need to pull him out of hiding and get him into the open."

"This person, whoever is shooting at us, clearly isn't the sharpest shooter, or they would have hit us by now." Troy looked over at her. "They're not a trained professional, but they obviously know enough about evasion to get away from a scene without getting caught."

"So? What are you trying to say?" She was utterly confused. "What do you want me to do? Stand up and flash the shooter?" she added, trying to make a joke in order to make the fear rising within her somewhat more manageable.

"Sure. I mean, if you took your shirt off and stood up, I think I could get out of this kitchen without him noticing. Then I could flank him, get the drop… We could get our man," he teased.

"What if it's a woman?"

Troy laughed. "Well, maybe I should take off my shirt… Do a little dance. She would love this rock-hard body."

"If it is a woman and you go up there without a shirt, it won't stop her from shooting—she'll just aim lower." Kate smirked. She reached into the drawer at the end of the counter and fished around until her fingers brushed against the cold metal of the flashlight. "Regardless, I think there are better options." She grabbed the flashlight as she pretended to lift her shirt.

"No. You keep covered," Troy ordered, no softness or questions in his tone. "There is absolutely no goddamned way I'm going to allow you to stand up and be shot at. There are a million better options."

"Don't worry. Not gonna get naked, but we gotta do something." She lifted the flashlight for him to see. "If we call in help, they'll just end up chasing him away. Like last time. You know we're on our own here." As much as she wanted to be wrong, she knew she was right.

Troy was silent.

"Cover my six, along with the rest of me. Get ready to run. I'm just going to do this one time." As it was, this one time was probably more than enough for her to end up dead. She clicked on the flashlight. "Go!"

She stood up and aimed the strobe in the direction of the shooter in hopes that the white flash would blind them. Looking to the left, up at the manor, she expected to see the muzzle flash, feel the pierce, then the burn of being struck with hot copper. The door outside clicked shut and she fell back down to the ground, clicking off the light and slipping it into her pocket.

Checking her body, she was surprised to find that the only real damage was still only to her ear. Lucky. This time, she had been right to act just a little bit crazy.

There was another crack and thump as the third round struck the microwave.

The jerk could ping her ear, shoot her flour, but

the bastard couldn't screw with her bacon. Moving to the island, she leaned out just far enough to take aim at the building in the distance. She was a good shooter, but if she hit the window where she believed the shooter to be, it would be one hell of a shot.

She fired three quick, successive rounds.

Though it had to have been excruciatingly loud in the small space of the kitchen, she hadn't even heard the sounds. The only reason she was entirely sure she had stopped at three rounds were the three spent casings on the ground to her right.

She turned her back against the island, catching her breath as she waited for the next round of shots.

Her breath came in short, fast bursts as she held her Glock to her chest, readying herself to roll and fire again. This jerk had to be stopped—and if something happened to Troy, she would stop at nothing when it came to finding this shooter and making them pay.

Chapter Sixteen

Troy turned the corner and ran to the front of the manor. It looked as though it had once been a bed-and-breakfast, but it now sat empty—except for, possibly, their shooter. The door's windows were covered with decades-old newspaper, all except the window closest to the handle and locks. The glass had been broken out at some point, but there were no shards on the ground in front of the door; either the pieces had been pushed into the building or it had happened long ago.

It wouldn't have surprised him if the place had come to serve as a high school rave location or some homeless hangout. Though this didn't seem the right kind of area for either, not with neighbors just a few hundred feet in every direction.

There was the flutter of a curtain as the resident across the street peeked out at him. He was tempted to wave, but he just made a mental note as he opened the unlocked door. No doubt, it would be only a matter of time until the police showed up, thanks to both the neighbor seeing him and Kate's shooting.

In the meantime, he had to get his hands on the dude who was trying to take them out. Once he did, the only thing that would be up for debate would be whether or not he chose to kill him.

The place smelled of stale air, mold and old cigarette smoke, all mixed with the carb-loaded aroma of cheap beer. He liked beer, but he'd always hated that odor.

The place had once probably been a nice dwelling, with its floral wallpaper, now stained with orange spray paint declaring "Donny loves Becca" in sloppy, dripping script. The brass chandelier overhead was at a slant and hanging from wires where a kid must have, at one time or another, tried to swing. In the right hands, the place had potential. But when he was done here, the next owner would need to know how to remove bloodstains.

He held his SIG, quickly clearing the entryway and living room before hurrying up the stairs, carefully avoiding the center of each step in order to mask the sounds of his advance. They couldn't know he was coming; he needed every advantage, especially when he held the lower ground.

Ascending the top of the staircase, he turned in the direction of the rooms that faced the back of Kate's house and her kitchen window. There were two possibilities, but he chose the one with the clearest view. Pressing his back to the wall, he sidestepped toward the open door. Taking a deep breath, he readied himself as he pivoted partially around the corner, making sure to remain behind the thin protection of the wall.

A man was sitting with his back to him at a small folding table, an assault rifle on a tripod and sandbags positioning the weapon toward Kate's kitchen window. He was dressed all in black and had on a backward black baseball hat, and a black-and-gray shemagh was wrapped around his neck; the only bit of skin showing were his ears and a bit of his cheeks. The masked man must have been some sort of trained shooter based on his choice of rifle and gear, but Troy was glad he wasn't better at his job. Or had he not been trying to kill Kate, but rather, had he just been trying to warn her off?

If he'd been serious, and well trained, he could have easily killed them both without them even realizing what was happening until it was all too late.

"Put your goddamned hands up, or you will get one straight to the brain stem." Troy roll-stepped behind the man, stopping only inches behind the back of his head.

The man didn't move. He didn't even flinch.

The wind whipped through the open window, blowing toward him; with it, it carried the coppery scent of blood. With the scent came a strange sense of unexpected disappointment.

"I said *put your hands up*," Troy repeated.

Still, the man didn't move.

He nudged the man's shoulder with the tip of his gun. His limp body collapsed to the floor. As he fell, he rolled, exposing an entrance wound just at the base of his throat.

Kate's aim had been on point.

She had killed the man.

Just when he thought he couldn't love her more, she had made what must have been at least a hundred-yard shot with a handgun, into a darkened room, and took down the bastard trying to kill her. It was a kill shot for the books.

What a woman.

He knelt down and checked the man's pulse, even though the open, sightless eyes told him all he needed to know. There was no sign of life.

Screw this fellow. He'd had it coming. The only thing that disappointed Troy was the fact that he hadn't been the one to pull the trigger, but he liked that the woman he loved had done it instead. She was powerful, smart and courageous.

They would make one hell of a team if they ever got married.

He paused as he stood up. What kind of person was he that, while checking on a dead man, he was thinking about getting married? And not just that, but he'd never really considered getting married before. Nope, it wasn't the kind of relationship he'd even contemplated, let alone hoped for…and yet here he was.

He couldn't help the smile that overtook his features as he moved out of the room, clearing the rest of the house. From what he could make out, there had been only this man. There was nothing to indicate he'd acted with anyone else.

Outside, there were the careening wails of police cruisers as they descended on him and the place.

Crap. Here we go again.

He considered leaving, but he hadn't done anything to conceal his fingerprints or his identity when the neighbor had spotted him. It was going to be easier just to face this head-on. But that didn't mean his ass wasn't going to be facing a little bit of jail time while he waited to be cleared.

Hopefully the investigating officer would be friendly toward him, maybe even throw him a couple of bones and let him walk. But Troy would have to get damn lucky.

He wished he'd had time to check the shooter's ID, but he had an idea of who he was. He put down his gun and walked outside. He plopped down on the porch's top step and waited until the first police car screeched and skidded to a stop in the street in front of him. The city officer stepped out of his car, using his door for coverage as he pulled his weapon and aimed it at him. "Get on the ground!"

He rolled over, pressed his face against the wooden planks. The paint was chipping and peeling, and he stared at a bit that fluttered as he exhaled and put his hands above his head, his fingers interlaced.

The police officer rushed toward him as two more

cars pulled up. The man patted him down, finding his holster. "Where is your weapon?"

Troy looked up at the man. "It's just inside the door. It's fully loaded. I just responded after the shooter shot at my girlfriend's place."

The police officer paused. "Where is your girlfriend?"

"Can I sit up?" Troy asked, being careful to not sound disrespectful.

"Keep your hands where I can see them and on your head. Got it?"

Troy nodded and the man pulled him up to sitting, using his interlaced hands. "My girlfriend is an FBI agent, and the man upstairs was trying to shoot and kill her. Her name is Kate Scot. She's with the Missoula field office."

The officer huffed and Troy wasn't sure if it was because the man was annoyed at Kate or annoyed at him. Hell, maybe he was annoyed that he had arrived two minutes too late.

"And what is your name? You FBI too?"

Troy laughed. "No. The name's Troy Spade. I'm a private contractor working with the Scot family." He carefully skirted the truth as much as he dared. The officer didn't need all the answers, at least not right now.

"The man upstairs is dead. I checked his pulse, but that was the extent of my interaction with him. He was already deceased when I got here."

"So you say." The officer pulled at his hands, motioning that he could relax. "You know why the dude was shooting at you and Kate?"

"I think this is the sniper from the downtown shooting last week, but that's yet to be proved. That being said, you probably know more about the investigation than I do."

The man holstered his weapon as several other officers descended on the house and the block and began clearing the area.

"You have reason to believe there are any other active shooters in the area?" the officer asked.

Troy shook his head, but then shrugged. "I cleared the house, but that doesn't mean there aren't others in the area. Right now, you need to send medical aid to Kate's place. She took a round, but it wasn't life-threatening. But the shooter got off more rounds while I was making my way over here. She shot back. I think she may have struck him. All self-defense," he added, making sure to protect her. He rattled off her address as the man called it in on his handset.

Troy needed to get back to her house and make sure that she was okay. "Can I go over there?"

The officer scoffed. "Yeah, right. Think again, Mr. Spade."

The only people who ever called him *Mr. Spade* were those about to rain down some sort of punishment on him. Hopefully he wasn't about to get his ass kicked or find himself heading to the clink.

"You know Kate?" he asked.

The officer nodded. "Good agent, good woman."

"I love her." Troy was shocked as the words fell from his lips. "I mean… I haven't told her that yet, but *I love her*, man. And I have to know she is okay. Have you ever loved a woman like that?"

The officer chuckled.

"If you have, then you have to know that even the threat of handcuffs and jail time isn't going to stop me from going over there and making sure that she's going to be okay. She's been through a lot. And if she is lying there on the floor of her kitchen, shot and bleeding…and I didn't do everything in my power to get to her, I would never forgive myself." He put his palms up, pleading.

"I don't know." The officer sighed.

"Look, the last woman I fell in love with ended up dead. EFP and caught shrapnel. I watched the whole thing go down. I can't stand the thought of losing another person I love. Not like that. Not like this. I can't… She can't be hurt."

The officer's face softened. "Here's the deal, Troy. I don't think you are the one responsible for the dead dude, but…you know there are procedures in place that require me to handle this a certain way. But… let's say you think that there is something *I have to see*, something at Kate's place… Well, I'm sure I can make it work."

Troy jumped to his feet, a smile stretching over his face. "I owe you one."

"More than one," the officer said. "And let me just say, you got it *bad* for Kate."

"Patsy Cline couldn't have sung it better, man. I know exactly how crazy I am for loving her. I just hope she is just as crazy about loving me."

The officer laughed, the sound out of place in the manic motions that were taking place around them.

Troy started jogging in the direction of Kate's house. "We were cooking… Well…*she* was cooking breakfast when the shooting began. Did you call EMS? They en route to her?" Troy's words came out fast as the officer jogged along next to him.

"They are en route." The officer started talking into his handset, letting the other officers know where he was and what he was doing.

As they rounded the corner, there were already two police cruisers and a black BuCar he recognized as Agent Hunt's.

He slowed down his race toward the front door as he thought about the dead man. He should have taken a second to get a better look at the guy's face. He thought he'd recognized him from Zoey's info dump, but wasn't quite sure. What if that guy was only one of a selection of snipers?

Snipers typically acted alone, but that didn't mean that they weren't part of a team. For the right amount of money, a person could buy anything—or have anyone killed, not limited to a captain of industry like Solomon Scot or an FBI agent like his daughter.

But who would be trying to take out the members of this family and why?

Maybe that first shooting had been about him

and his brother, and not about Kate, as he'd first suspected. This second shooting, though, had been about her.

Someone was working sloppy here. It was like whoever was at the wheel and driving these attacks wasn't used to doing this kind of work, but had one hell of a budget.

That left Peahen out. An agent made good money, but they didn't make that kind of money. And even if Peahen was getting paid by someone else, he was smart enough not to play sniper. Too many risks. It just didn't fit his MO.

The only people connected to the case, the ones with enough money to make a sniper happen—at least, the only ones he could think of—were those who were associated with ConFlux. Maybe there was someone on the board, someone who didn't want them to come under investigation for leaked secrets... That would explain why he and Mike had been shot at. And it definitely explained why someone would shoot and kill Solomon.

But why would they come after him and Kate?

Were they getting too close to the answers? Did someone need to stop Troy and Kate before being exposed?

Then again, the other two suspects both worked for ConFlux, and either could have been the sniper. And if one of them was the dead man in the manor, it was possible that he'd been working alone. Maybe he'd been the one selling secrets.

Kate had said Sal was one of her father's new hires. That moved him to the top of his personal suspects list. Damn—he wished he'd taken a picture of the dead shooter. He'd resembled Sal, but Zoey's photo of him had been of a younger man, probably something taken earlier. Maybe he was working for a foreign government—a spy of some sort. Hell, it made sense.

Zoey was probably having a tech field day with all of this.

His mind was working a million miles an hour as he ran around to the open back door and made his way into the kitchen. The officer with him had pulled his weapon, and Troy appreciated the effort as the officer pushed past him and took point so they would both be protected if they unexpectedly came under fire.

There were voices coming from the living room. Standing at the center was Kate. Agent Hunt had a bottle of hydrogen peroxide and was swabbing her ear with a rag. Troy pushed him aside.

"Kate," Troy said, taking her by the shoulders and looking her square in the eyes. "Are you okay? You didn't get hit anywhere else, did you? You're fine, right?" His words flooded from him as he looked her over, spinning her slightly as he looked for anywhere that could have been hurt.

The only thing that appeared injured was the tip of her ear, where only a small patch of skin was missing.

She smiled, relieved, and threw her arms around his neck. "Troy, I'm fine. Honey, it's okay. It's going to be okay."

He breathed in her scent, pulling the smell of pancakes and her shampoo deep into his lungs. But beneath the soft aromas of her was the heady scent of fear. No matter what she said, or what she swore to, Kate was still afraid.

Chapter Seventeen

Kate had killed a man. The locals had identified him as Sal Baker, an employee of ConFlux. Though they had a few answers, and the ballistics were all being handled by the FBI lab so they could get more, there were still too many questions, and only one real thought kept circulating through her mind… She had taken a person's life two days ago.

When she had taken on her role as a special agent with the Bureau, she had known that someday she would likely be faced with a situation in which she would have to possibly take a life. She had trained for hundreds of hours at the range over the years, to the point that calluses formed at the base of her thumb where her Glock's beavertail rubbed against her skin every time she pulled the trigger.

Yes, she was proficient with a handgun—more than capable, even—but she just couldn't get over the reality that she had taken aim at a nearly invisible target, pulled that trigger and made the kill shot on her enemy.

She didn't regret her actions. Not when the man was trying to kill them. Troy had made a point of saying that he was there to protect her, and she secretly loved the fact that when push had come to shove, she was the one who had protected him.

Maybe, in the future, if they were to really pursue a grown-up relationship, they could even face it together with some sort of pride.

She would never forget the look on his face when he had found her standing in the living room... He'd seemed absolutely at a loss. Relieved, yes, but at the same time like he had never been more terrified in his entire life.

In that moment, she had wanted to make him forget everything bad that had ever happened to him, and though she knew that not everything he had to have been feeling was tied to her, she wanted to take away all of his pain. If only she could. He had so many burdens, and they made all the seemingly terrible and heart-wrenching things that had ever happened to her pale in comparison. Really, what was a breakup in comparison to watching a loved one die?

Her father's murder came slamming back into her consciousness. For a split second, she had forgotten. How had she failed to recall the pain of losing him? Of seeing his body being wheeled out of his office building?

Did it make her a terrible person that all she had been really thinking about was what she and Troy had just gone through?

She stared at the far wall of her office. Though the SAC, Agent Raft, had told her to take the day off and stay home, focus on her family, it was the last thing she had wanted to do. Every time she peeked at her phone, there were messages from her mother, her sister and restricted numbers that she was more than sure belonged to the detectives and officers who were working on the task force and trying to solve all of these murders.

Agent Hunt walked up beside her desk and tossed down a bag of sunflower seeds. "Here, champ, have one on me."

She laughed as she picked up the bag. "Thanks, man."

"You doing okay?" he asked.

His question surprised her. He didn't usually pry or ask questions when it came to anything beyond work. They were friends, but they both respected the fact that neither delved too deep. Both knew exactly what they needed to know about each other, and beyond that, anything else was only a liability.

She nodded, opening the bag and stuffing a few seeds into the back of her cheek like they were some kind of pacifier. "Doing fine. One day at a time, am I right?"

Hunt nodded. He paused and an awkward silence moved between them.

"Something you wanted to tell me, Hunt?"

He sat half on the corner of her desk. If anyone else did that, she would have been annoyed, but she liked Hunt too much to give a damn. He took in a deep breath, as if he was trying to decide whether or not he wanted to divulge a secret.

"Just say it." She couldn't stand to think about what other shoe was about to drop.

"I know you and Troy are…well, getting *close*."

She clenched. Since when did everyone know about her personal relationship? As soon as she asked herself the question, she realized that everyone in the entire city probably knew by now. Their story, the shooting and the sniper's death had been the talk of every news outlet in the state for the last forty-eight hours, and she doubted that would stop anytime soon.

She and Troy hadn't seen each other since then. She had a lot to do in the aftermath of the shooting, and he'd texted her several times telling her he was happy to give her some space.

She'd been careful to avoid watching any of the news coverage, but from what she had managed to glean, most media sources hadn't seemed to say much about the nature of her and Troy's friendship. But anyone who knew her knew exactly what had transpired—especially Hunt, who had borne witness to *the look* Troy had given her when he'd first seen her after the shooting.

That look told her everything she needed to know about how Troy felt…and she felt it too. Though she hadn't seen her own features, she was absolutely certain that she had been his mirror.

"Are you jealous, Hunt?" she teased, though she was more than aware that Agent Hunt had a girl-friend.

"Hardly. You and I are many things. Romantically inclined toward one another, we are not. But don't think I wouldn't take a bullet for you," Hunt said, his voice unwavering and true.

"So, what, then?" she asked, giving him a play-ful half smile.

"Well, in an effort to take a bullet for you—I think I need to tell you something, before you get too hurt because of this thing with Troy."

Her stomach dropped and she was pretty sure every single drop of blood had just flooded into her feet. "Okay… What about him?"

Hunt sucked in a breath, letting it out in a slow, metered exhalation. "So, I have been looking into him ever since the shooting downtown. I know he's your friend, but has he told you anything about his past?"

She thought about his accident. "What about his past?"

"Well, you know he has been working private contracting?"

"Yes. He's currently with STEALTH. What about it?"

"Did he tell you which company he worked with before that?" Hunt's face pinched.

She shook her head.

"It was a company called Rockwood. You ever heard of it?"

"No. Why?" A sickening lump formed in her throat.

"Rockwood is a private contracting group. They work under the United Nations and are a big-time billion-dollar company that not many people in the public sector could name." Hunt crossed his arms over his chest, leaning back slightly. "Your boy worked for them for quite a few years, doing what—I couldn't find, but I'm sure with a few more phone calls I could at least get some basics."

She tried to swallow back the lump. "These guys, who work in the trade... There's a lot of lateral movements between outfits. What's your point?"

Hunt sucked on his teeth. "Well, that guy you put down, Sal Baker, he worked for that outfit as well. You don't think he was aiming at Troy all along, do you? Or—" Hunt paused "—you don't think that Troy and/or his team are playing us all for fools, do you?"

She laughed at the outrageous conjecture. "That's crazy, Hunt. Seriously, that's a bit of a stretch, don't you think? That's like saying you're more loyal to your first boss than the Bureau."

He answered with the quirk of an eyebrow. "Is it? I've been thinking about it...and here is this guy who has admitted to trying to break into ConFlux. What if he and Sal were working together?"

The lump grew larger. "No..."

"Did he or did he not get you to walk him up to your father's office?"

She had. Kate had literally opened the door and gotten him waved past security. Who knew what he had done when he'd been alone in the intern's office?

"Okay, let's say they were working for the same team. Why would Sal bear down on us in my kitchen?"

"*Us?* Or you?"

There was some validity in what Hunt was saying, but she refused to admit the possibility that Troy would act in any way that would go against her. It wasn't possible. Not after what had happened between them—after how he had made her feel.

Or had he been using her heart against her? Had she been honeypotted by the man?

She ran her finger over the scab that had formed where she had been hit by the sniper's round. Troy had convinced her that Sal wasn't a great sniper, and she had gone along with it—what kind of sniper couldn't hit their target at around a hundred yards? It shouldn't have been a very difficult shot, and even an amateur shooter could have made it.

Though they had all discussed the logistics of the shooter's trajectory and path, the task force and investigating officer had agreed that it was likely a case of a poor-quality shooter. But what if that wasn't what had happened after all? What if she was only supposed to get a notch in the ear?

Had Troy treated her like a lamb and brought her to the slaughter?

Her entire body turned cold, but she wasn't sure if it was out of sheer terror or rage. "I need to go." She stood up, leaving her suit jacket on the back of her chair. "Oh, and call Peahen. I need to talk to him. I think I owe him an apology."

"Why? Wait—do you want me to come with you?" Hunt called after her.

"No." She didn't need a witness if she lost it on the one man outside the agency whom she had chosen to give her trust to.

This was what she got for opening up to a man. When would she learn her lesson and just get a dog and not try to go for the whole relationship package? This had all been too quick. She should have known better, been more cautious.

She took out her phone as she walked from the federal building and made her way to her car. Pushing the buttons, she dialed Troy. He had better answer his damn phone.

It rang, finally going to voice mail.

Her rage burned hotter, melting through what little self-restraint she still possessed. When she found him, he was going to not only get a piece of her mind, but he was probably going to get a swift throat punch right along with it.

But first, she had to find him.

How was it that when she didn't think she needed him, he was just around the corner, but now that she wanted to find him, he had gone completely dark?

As she made it to the car, she wasn't sure where

she should start looking for Troy. Would he still be at STEALTH headquarters? For all she knew, like Hunt had implied, he had used her for what he needed and now he had already bugged out.

Then again, Zoey had vouched for him. Or he had said Zoey had vouched for him. Had that been a lie too? She hadn't *actually talked* to her or anyone else in STEALTH.

But her father had vouched for him and his brother… And was Mike his brother? Had anything he told her about himself been true? Had his girl-friend even been killed?

What if all he had been doing was manipulating her as he tried to get what he needed for his assign-ment or for whatever purpose he had in mind?

An icy chill ran down her spine.

No. She had to stop swirling the drain. Hunt had to be wrong.

But now that he had pointed out his suspicions, she couldn't help but follow her thoughts to the inky dark-ness of what Troy could have been doing. The farther she drove, the angrier she became.

By the time she was bumping down the dirt road that led to the Widow Maker Ranch, where STEALTH's headquarters was located, she was seething. She pulled the car to a skidding stop in the gravel parking lot and charged toward the ranch house's front door.

Using the mammoth cast-iron lion's head knocker, she banged on the door. The sound echoed out into the still morning. A cow bawled in the distance, the only one who dared to answer. There was an electronic whir as a camera moved overhead and the aperture moved to focus.

She knocked again.

"I'm coming," a woman called from the other side of the door. There were the sounds of footfalls and a metal slide. Zoey, her hair a dark purple, opened the door. "What are you doing here, Agent Scot? Is there something I can help you with this morning?"

She charged into the house. "Where is Troy?"

"Um, excuse me? What are you doing? What did *he* do?" Zoey slammed the door shut and chased after her, grabbing her by the arm and spinning her around so they were facing one another. "What happened?"

"Did you know that he used to work for Rockwood?" she spit.

Zoey frowned. "What about it? Several of our employees have worked for Rockwood in the past."

"I think they all may still be working for them. Are you in on this?" She nearly growled as she stared at the dark eyeliner that made Zoey's eyes appear catlike.

"What in the hell are you talking about?"

"Troy!" she yelled, pulling out of Zoey's grasp. "Troy! Where in the hell are you?"

Zoey jogged beside her as she charged down the hallway toward what looked like the bedrooms. "You have to tell me what is going on."

"Why don't you just tell me where Troy is? Then he can tell *both* of us what he is doing and why."

Zoey pointed toward a door at the end of the hall.

Kate rushed in that direction, and not bothering to knock, she threw open the bedroom door.

Troy was just starting to sit up. He wasn't wearing a shirt, and as he spotted her, he moved his hand away from the nightstand where his holster rested.

"Don't you dare lay a finger on that gun, or your friend Sal won't be the only one who I put a bullet into this week," Kate ordered.

Zoey grabbed her hand, flipping it behind her back and pinning it upward. "Look, I don't know what is going on here, but there is no way I'm going to let you charge into our headquarters and draw down on one of my employees. We have one rule here—no shooting in the house."

Troy put his hands up, shock registering on his features. "What is going on, Kate? What are you doing here?"

"Did you really think I wasn't going to find out about your past? What you are really up to?" She turned to Zoey. "Did you know that your boy here has ties to the sniper who *allegedly* tried to kill him and Mike? It's all an effing setup. And I was the fool who fell for it."

Zoey opened her mouth as she glanced over at Troy and then back to her, as though she was trying to make sense of all the things that Kate was saying. "Are you talking about Rockwood?" she asked, finally finding the words.

"Rockwood?" Troy asked, rubbing the sleep from his face. "Dude, I haven't worked for them in years."

"Don't lie. You may not be working for Rockwood, but you asked Sal to do what he did." There was the burn of tears as they started to collect in her eyes. "You never thought he would get hurt. You never thought I would take that shot. That I would make that shot. I killed a man. All because you and STEALTH wanted to get access to my family's company."

"What?" Troy frowned and his lips parted—he looked absolutely confused.

He was a gifted liar. He had to have known exactly what she was talking about. Or maybe she was wrong and she had flown off the deep end.

No. She was right. Everything pointed in this direction.

"If you're not in on this, then what in the hell is going on? If it walks like a duck, talks like a duck—it's a goddamned duck. You are a duck." She felt stupid as soon as she said it, but in her stressed state, she had a hard time coming up with anything eloquent. All she could focus on was her own pain in falling for the wrong man.

Why had she strayed from her Bureau training? The training that tried to impress upon them that everything anyone ever did was always selfishly motivated. Troy had done what he needed to do to get the answers that he needed. It was all about him, and she had forgotten about that, letting herself get swept away by the ill-advised belief that he cared about her.

As the tears threatened to leak through, she turned and charged out of the room. He couldn't see her cry again. She needed to get herself back into check, compartmentalize her feelings—especially any that were about him.

After arriving back at her car, she pressed her forehead against the steering wheel and counted to ten, pinching back the tears.

This was going to be okay.

She was going to be okay.

Sure, she had made a mistake in getting involved with Troy. But maybe there was some kind of positive outcome that she could draw from it… What had he taught her?

Her mind drew a blank. All she could think about was the ache within her.

At Quantico, they had taught her that there were two driving factors in everyone's psyche—love and fear. It was what motivated every single action a person took. Even hate could come back to love. Rage could come back to fear. And when a person mixed these two simple concepts, no weapon could be more deadly.

At the time during training, she had thought she had understood what her instructors had meant, but now…in this situation, the true visceral, terrifying truth of what they had said struck home.

She could never get in another relationship again. It was so much easier being alone, walls around her feelings and the sentinels of aloofness standing guard at her gates.

Chapter Eighteen

Kate's house was empty, the yellow tape still fluttering in the breeze like it was celebrating the desecration of their lives last night. He wasn't sure he had ever seen a more morose object, and it struck him how something so mundane could carry so much meaningful pain.

Troy had to find her. He had to set things right. To tell her everything about him and open up in as many ways as he could.

As good as he was at being a shadow, trying to find her this morning just proved to him that she was equally as qualified and adept at his kind of games—two shadows brought together could bring only darkness. And right now, he found himself restless in the inky black. Though he had vowed he would never let himself get to this point again, here he was. At least this time there was a slight glow of light at the edge of the darkness: hope. But with each passing second, the glimmer diminished.

Zoey's name popped up on his phone, and with

it came a text message. She had spotted Kate's car downtown, near the federal building. She was parked in front of a bookstore called Fact & Fiction and was probably inside.

He knew the place and turned the car around, hitting the gas like he was bearing down on a fugitive— fighting for the love of his life was similar in a number of ways. Each was equally terrifying, and in both instances, lives depended on the outcome of his actions.

Kate's car was parked exactly where Zoey had pinpointed it, and not for the first time, he thanked his lucky stars. Parking on the street near the car, he got out and made his way to the bookstore. There was a note on the door: Closed.

About right. So much for things being easy.

It gnawed at him that he didn't know Kate well enough to figure out where she would go when she was upset. Did it mean that he didn't really love her? That what he was feeling was merely infatuation? Lust?

If that was all it was, then why hadn't her rushing into his bedroom and falsely accusing him of a crime put a stop to his feelings? And by rushing him, that had to mean she had feelings for him too, right? Otherwise, she wouldn't have tipped her hand and gone at him directly.

That had to mean something, didn't it? She had to have some sort of feelings, the kind that would make her bend rules and act against her better judgment. Which only meant one thing: love.

Though, it all could have been hopeful thinking.

Kate was probably just angry and not thinking straight. Then again, she was a better agent than that. He couldn't blame her for being upset or thinking what she did of him. He could understand the thought process that could have gotten her to where she was, but he had to talk her down. He had to bring her back to reality. She was fighting her biggest ally.

If only he had the answers to why her father had been murdered and if it was truly Sal who was behind it. With Zoey's help, he'd followed some leads that had turned up only the obvious, that Sal had tried to steal info. If he knew more, he could prove that everything he had told her was true and that he was the man she needed in her life—not an enemy and certainly not someone who wanted to hurt her.

The street was quiet. The only other person was walking toward him, posting flyers on the light poles and traffic lights. The paper had a picture of a lost dog.

Turning left, he made his way down the block, peeking into the variety of sandwich shops, clothing stores and coffee shops as he looked for Kate. He walked to the end of the strip of downtown buildings and was going to turn and head back toward her car to wait for her to return, but as he neared an alleyway, he spotted a gray sedan parked in the shade of the building.

Inside the car were a man and woman. The man had his hand wrapped around the back of the woman's head, and even from where Troy stood, he could feel the intensity of their kiss. He felt oddly out of place for even noticing their embrace. As he watched, the man looked up at him and broke away from the woman, flattening his hair and stroking his goatee. There was a mole near his left temple, and it twitched as the man looked up at him, eyes widened with surprise and a thin sweat on his face. Guilt.

The woman turned around and, as she did, Troy recognized her brunette eyes and bobbed platinum gray hair. Deborah Scot looked much like an older version of her daughter. His gaze slipped back to the man—no wonder the man had looked shocked to see him.

He turned around, quickly moving out of their line of sight before one of them recognized him. Not that they would have known who he was, even if they had actually taken note of him as more than anything other than a passing observer.

But what exactly had he just seen? They had definitely been kissing. No question. Which meant there was a relationship there. He didn't recognize the man, but it didn't matter. Troy had just found a motive for murder.

He hurried down the sidewalk, putting as much distance between him and his targets as possible. He didn't need to be the next one to end up dead.

Where was Kate? He had to find her. Taking out his phone, he ducked into the nearest door and walked into the busy coffee shop. It smelled of cinnamon and fresh-baked rolls mixed with the burnt caffeinated aroma of coffee.

He dialed Kate.

Answer. You need to answer.

It went to voice mail. It took three more attempts before she finally picked up. "What do you want?"

So, she is still pissed. Not a surprise.

"I need you to come meet me. I'm at The Break." He spoke fast. "It's important. Seriously."

Kate scoffed. "Are you kidding me? There is no way I'm going to meet—"

"I just spotted your mother in an alley kissing a man," he interrupted her, not waiting for her to come at him with more vinegar. "Now. Get your ass over here."

There was a long pause.

"I'll be there in a minute." The anger was stripped from her voice.

He stood awkwardly for a moment. A woman sitting nearest the window was looking at him, so he walked to the counter and ordered a hot tea and a cup of coffee for Kate. He paid and they handed him his cups. He added cream and sugar to hers, making it just how she liked it, before moving to the back corner of the room and finding a table away from the rest of the patrons. He folded his napkin until the bell on the door jingled, and he slipped the crane away.

Kate walked in, and as she spotted him, a frown took over her face.

Yep, still mad.

He stood up as she approached the table, but her eyes darkened to the point of nearly black. One of these days he would really try to get things right with her.

"First," he said, motioning for her to sit. "I want to tell you that I understand where you are coming from. You're a good agent, and your father's case is still open. You are right to be suspicious of everybody. But I swear to all that is good in this world that I have absolutely nothing to do with any of what has happened to you."

"Then why were you so adamant about getting close to me, protecting me?" Her frown lessened, like she was truly trying to understand his motivation. "You know that's abnormal. Most people don't go out of their way for someone else. No one is selfless. That is a myth."

Unless they wholeheartedly love the other person.

Right now, it didn't seem like the right moment to point that out, so he tried stepping around the admission. "I know what you mean. And I know you are leery of trusting me or anyone right now, but if you give me a chance, I will prove to you that I'm worthy of your trust. I only want…" *To love you. To marry you. To have a future with you. To keep you safe.*

There were a million things he wanted with this woman, but he didn't know which thing he should say.

"You want to prove yourself?" she asked, skeptically.

"Exactly." He nodded, feeling like a castigated

schoolboy. "It's why I called you. Why I had to talk to you about your mother. I couldn't just let you find out on your own. Regardless of how it made you feel, you have to know the truth. That, that ability to give another the truth even when it hurts, is *trust*. Isn't it?"

"Perhaps your candor helps, but it doesn't make any of this an easier pill to swallow."

"I know, Kate, and I'm so sorry I have to be the bearer of the bad news, but I promise I will stand by your side as long as you need me. We will get to the bottom of your father's murder—and the role your mother may or may not have played in it."

She gave a resigned sigh. "You said you saw her *kissing* someone?" She made a disgusted face as she sat down across from him at the table and took the cup of coffee he offered. "Thank you." She took a long sip like it was a salve for the wounds to her heart—if only he could be that for her too.

He yearned to reach out and take her hand, but he restrained himself. Right now, he needed to focus on proving himself. "Do you know a guy, gray hair, mole near the left temple?"

She looked up and to her right, trying to recall an image. "There is a guy. I think his name was Alex or Alexi or something. He worked for ConFlux. I think he was the head of the IT department."

Oh, holy... He'd struck pay dirt.

"Hold on," he said, motioning to Kate to keep that thought as he gestured for her to go with him.

He stood up from the table, taking out his phone

and dialing Zoey. She answered before he'd even gotten to the front door of the place.

"What's the name of the guy who is the head of IT for ConFlux?" He walked outside, Kate close at his heels.

"Alexi Siegal. Why?"

"I want everything you can pull on the guy. See if he's dropped any out-of-place or nonrequired code on their servers." Troy's mind worked quickly as he thought about all the things he would do if he was Alexi. "Make sure to watch all major airlines. I have a feeling that if this guy catches wind of us being on his tail, he's going to disappear. Wouldn't even be a bad idea if you had our people put out a BOLO on this guy."

"What are you talking about?" Zoey asked. "What did Alexi do?"

"He and Deborah Scot are having an affair. That might explain how this whole bonfire was set ablaze." Even to his own ears, he sounded breathless.

"Oh, I'm on it." The phone went dead as Zoey hung up.

Ah, Zoey, that beautiful, beautiful soul.

Kate jogged so she was walking beside him as he strode back toward his car. "Where are you going?"

"I don't know." He stopped. He was sure that her mother and her lover were long gone by now, thanks to his spotting them. Luckily, neither of them would have known him—the ghost. "Who is the beneficiary of your father's will?"

"I'm sure it's my mother. Do you think she was behind his death?"

He scrunched his face as he spoke, not wanting Kate to face the pain of her mother being involved in her father's murder. "She might be guilty of something. She and this guy, this Alexi. But we are going to have to prove it. Do you think you could get me back into the ConFlux building?"

"I'm sure, but what do you think you are going to find? So far, none of the people the police interviewed have had any information. And there hasn't been a whisper of my mother…my mother having… you know…an *affair.*" She said the word like it was filled with worm guts. "Are you sure you saw what you saw?"

"I'm sure." He hated that he had to push this thing in her face, especially so soon after her father's death, but there was no avoiding what he had seen. "Are you close with your mother?"

She swallowed what must have been a lump in her throat, and even he could tell she was struggling to get past it.

He reached out, hoping and praying that she would slip her hand into his. He needed to know that she would have faith in him, that she had put her suspicions about him aside. Especially with the new information.

She didn't move.

He dropped his hand by his side. "Maybe your mother and Alexi are still there." It was unlikely, but right now his word wasn't going to make her believe him. In a case like this, with so much at stake, the only thing she would trust was going to be what she saw with her own two eyes. He couldn't blame her. *Doveryáy, no proveryáy.*

Instead of waiting for her to take his hand, he slipped his fingers into hers. He couldn't make her feel anything, he couldn't make her trust him, but he could prove himself to her. As they made their way to the alley, he peeked around the corner. The car was gone. He stopped.

Crap.

He'd taken a chance not following them, but it had been a calculated risk to keep them from knowing he was on their tail. He had to find them, to stop them from getting out of the city and the state. Once they did, it would be a hell of a lot harder to pin them down and bring them to justice.

"This is where they were?" Kate asked, her voice flecked with annoyance.

"Yeah, but don't worry. They couldn't have gone far. And Zoey is working on putting out a BOLO." He reached over and took her hand, giving it a reassuring squeeze. "I know how hard this must be for you, but I've got you. We are in this together."

"Just as long as we find them. That's what matters now."

They stood there for a moment in tense silence as he dissected her words. He didn't want to tell her that there were many things that mattered more—

namely, the way he felt about her and what he wanted for their future—but thankfully she hadn't let go of his hand. Maybe she was starting to forgive him for being the messenger.

He wished he could open up and tell her that he loved her, but right now…it wasn't right. When he finally let those words come out of his mouth, he wanted it to be perfect—if there was such a thing. She deserved to be told in a way that would create a memory she'd cherish. She was special and she deserved to be treated like the goddess that she was.

"Let's jump in and head toward the interstate," she said, motioning toward his car. "Maybe we can catch them heading toward Idaho."

If he was trying to bug out, that would be his objective as well. More populous areas to get lost in, and no international border to cross. Though, he would never have been stupid enough to get onto the one interstate that ran nearly the entire length of the state. He would take the back roads, the logging roads that led to Idaho and would keep him far outside the sites of any law enforcement. The only thing a person would have to worry about on those roads would be a game warden. As luck had it, there were only two who worked in this county. The odds would ever be in his favor.

Then again, Deborah and Alexi, a desk-jockey tech geek, didn't seem like the types who would head out to the woods or anywhere that lacked high-end amenities. If anything, they seemed like the airport kind of people. They wouldn't want to merely leave the state—they had assets that most didn't, including a deep set of pockets.

And with deep pockets came endless resources. A person could get anything for the right amount of money. In fact, he had once had a boss at the UN who had requested he do something nearly impossible that required several NDAs and a threat of death. When Troy had tried to tell the man no and that it couldn't be done, the man had told him just to give him the number of zeros it would take on the check to make it happen.

It had taken some work, but his mission had been accomplished. And, as luck had it, the perfect number of zeros on the check was seven. Immense requests required immense bank accounts—luckily, that was something his contact at the UN had in spades.

Thinking back on it, he really didn't miss those days.

He opened the car door for Kate and she slipped into the passenger seat. And though she was safely tucked away with him, he hated having to stop touching her. As soon as he got in and was buckled, he put out his hand and waited until she slipped her fingers into his before he took to the road.

Turning off Broadway, he took to the interstate in the direction of the airport, soon pulling off on the exit.

"Where are we going?" she asked, surprised.

"I bet you twenty bucks that she is at the airport.

That or they are renting a private jet at Minuteman. Let's start here."

Kate opened her mouth like she was thinking about arguing. She'd tried calling her mom but it had gone straight to voice mail. Either the woman didn't have her phone or wasn't picking up.

"Besides, we are not going to stop them even if they are on the interstate. MHP will have to catch up to them if they are going that way. At the very least, if they are trying to cross over to Idaho, there is only one point they can do that from the interstate. If I was an officer, I would be sitting ten miles before that state line, waiting. We're covered."

She gripped his hand tighter, and from her touch he could sense her frustration—he didn't blame her. With so much riding on them finding her mom, it was hard not to feel like they had her father's memory pressing down on them—not to mention the fate of her family's company. A company that for all intents and purposes would likely belong to her once her mother was found and faced justice if she'd been involved in her husband's murder.

Luckily the airport was only a few minutes away—even less the way he drove. He pulled to a stop in front of the doors leading to the main terminal, not caring whether or not their car would be towed.

As he was about to put the car in Park, his phone pinged with a message.

Zoey's text was simple: Targets just entered airport.

"They're trying to catch a flight," Troy ordered,

excited that his assumption had been spot-on. He would have liked to think he was just that good, but there was no doubt that half of this was luck.

Getting out of the car, they rushed into the main body of the airport. An airport police officer was standing beside the boarding pass kiosks, his hands over his chest and a stoic look on his face. Troy hurried over to him. "Hey, there is a BOLO out on a man and woman, late fifties, early sixties, gray haired. Have you seen them?"

The man dropped his arms from his chest and snorted a laugh. "You just described about half the people in this airport."

Kate flashed him her badge. "We need information on this couple as quickly as possible. They are involved in a murder investigation." She lifted up her phone, showing him a picture of her mother. "This is the woman. Man has a mole on the left side of his face, near the temple."

The man took a close look at the woman. Grabbing his handset and turning away from them, he called the other officers on duty. It took a couple of minutes while the officer talked in a truncated, coded conversation before he turned back to them. "From our video feed, they were in the airport about five minutes ago. Then went back out to the long-term parking lot. We don't have any record of them leaving the property."

They were still on the grounds. "Close down all the public exits. We need to make sure that they can't escape. And we need you to call in to the locals, let them know what we have here."

The officer nodded. "We're already on it. Unfortunately, there is only myself and another officer on duty, but we will work as efficiently as possible."

Kate gave him a tip of the head. "Great. We'll start in long-term."

Troy gave him a clipped description of the car and the license plate number, though they were already a part of the BOLO. "You guys work short-term and the toll booth areas. If you come in contact, let us know."

They jogged out of the terminal. Their car was still running in front and they got back in. Hurrying around the loop, they entered the long-term parking lot. It wasn't a huge area, but there were only a few open parking spaces. And, as they twisted through the lot, he noted three other sedans that matched the car he had seen in the alleyway, but not the license plate.

As they rounded the second-to-last row, he spotted the car. It was still running. He parked in front of the nose of the vehicle, blocking them in, stopping them from escaping.

Kate jumped out of the car, her gun at the ready, pointed in the direction of the driver's seat. The man with the gray hair sat there, gesticulating wildly, almost as if the two were having some sort of fight. They didn't even notice them bearing down.

Her mother was in the passenger seat, and though

Troy couldn't hear what she was saying, he could tell she was yelling. As he and Kate approached the car, neither Deborah nor Alexi looked over. Whatever was going on was heated.

He unholstered his SIG Sauer, readying himself just in case all of this went south. Though he hoped the two would see the futility of their situation, desperation led to desperate and often dangerous choices; choices a person wouldn't normally make.

Kate carefully approached the driver's-side door and knocked on the window, pulling the man's attention away from her mother and directly to her. The man jerked like he hadn't noticed anything outside of the world that he had built with Deborah.

Troy watched the man's hands, his right moving toward his ankle as the left moved to roll down the window.

"Put your hands where I can see them!" Troy ordered, pointing his gun at Alexi, backing Kate.

The man jerked as the window rolled down. "Whoa. I just had an itch—don't worry. There's nothing going on here, at least nothing you need to worry about. Stand down." He sneered over at Troy, his voice dismissive.

"What are you doing here, Kate?" Deborah asked. Her hair was mussed, her lipstick smeared. Her makeup was streaked where tears had slipped down and disappeared.

"I'm wondering the same thing about you, Mom." Kate growled, nudging the barrel of her gun in the man's direction. "Alexi, you need to step out of the vehicle."

The man's hands moved to the steering wheel.

"Put your hands up!" Troy yelled, afraid that if the man took the wheel, he would do something stupid.

Kate stepped back, as if she too was worried that the man would punch the gas and ram their car.

Alexi chuckled, raising his hands. "I know how this probably looks to you guys, but your mother and I were just talking. She's been through a lot and—"

"Stop right there," Kate said, as she walked over and, leaning in through the car's window, turned off the engine, removing the keys. She stuffed the keys into her pocket. "You can lie to some people, but I'm not one of them. I know exactly what you two are up to, and don't think you can get away with it. Now, both of you need to step out of the damn car, or we will remove you from this vehicle."

Her mother reached down and touched the door handle, moving to get out.

"No," Alexi said. "Deborah, you stay exactly where you are. They have no right to tell us to do anything. And I don't know where they're getting off trying to order us around like we're some kind of fugitives."

Kate laughed, the sound dangerous and low. "Really? You think you can play that game with me? If you don't get out of this car right now, I'll make sure I have every police officer from here to Seattle on your ass."

Alexi laughed. "For what?"

There were a few moments in life that Troy hated. The worst was inarguably facing death. Then came moments like this… Moments in which two people who loved each other were forced to see the other for who they really were. Humans could be the ugliest, most despicable and cruel creatures in existence.

Though he had no doubt that her mother loved her, Deborah was quite possibly a murderer. Regardless of the love that she held for her mother, Kate would have to do what her job dictated no matter how much it hurt. And what made it all worse was the fact that Kate held the cuffs, ones that could place her mother behind bars possibly until her dying day.

Chapter Nineteen

Kate could've been sick.

Here she had been, completely convinced that Troy was her enemy. And now here she was, forced to face the fact that her enemy was the one person she thought she could trust. Sure, she and her mother had never been entirely close, but her mom had loved her. And she thought her mother and father had, for the most part, gotten along. Maybe they hadn't had the strongest marriage that she'd ever seen, but in the lineup of corporate men and corporate wives, they seemed stable.

She couldn't imagine what had pushed her mother to have an affair. Troy had made it clear that he thought her mother was behind her father's murder, but she wasn't entirely sure. Not yet. There were any number of possibilities. One thing was certain, however: her mother hadn't pulled the trigger. Though she hadn't gotten the fingerprint analysis and ballistics tests back, she was almost certain that her mother's prints wouldn't be on any of the shell casings.

"If you don't get out of the car right now, we will drag your asses out." She paused. "I just got my nails done and I really don't want to get physical, but if you make me, Alexi, I'll be more than happy to facilitate."

Alexi moved to say something, but her mother stopped him with a touch to his arm. "Just listen to her."

Alexi sighed.

Her mother and Alexi slowly stepped out of the vehicle, closing the doors behind them.

Troy visibly relaxed. Apparently, he had thought things were going to go haywire. Though she should've been focusing on her own emotional turmoil, finding her mother in such a compromising position, all she could feel was a little bit satisfied that she'd pegged her mother's reaction right.

Her mother wasn't perfect—she was an adult, and she was human, but she wasn't evil. Maybe she had just gotten herself in a situation that she couldn't get out of. Maybe she had been forced to make a choice between something crappy and something crappier. That was how most crimes happened. Not that she was making excuses for her mother. She was only trying to understand.

"I want you both to go and sit on the hood of this vehicle," Kate ordered, reminding herself that this was work and not merely some screwed-up family drama.

Alexi and her mother walked to the front of the

car and sat down. Troy strode over toward them. "You want me to pat them down?"

She nodded. Though she knew she should go help him, there was something so very wrong about her going to look for weapons on her mother and her boyfriend. Instead, she took out her phone and set it on the top of the car, recording their conversation.

"Mrs. Scot, can you please turn around and spread your legs?" Troy motioned toward the front of the car. "I'm going to pat you down now. Do you have anything in your pockets that could potentially stab or cut me? Do you have any sort of weapon that I need to know about?"

Her mother shook her head.

"Mom, do you want to tell me how Sal was involved in all of this?" she asked, hoping that her mother would answer her honestly while she was in such a compromising position. "It's better for you if you do." She proceeded to give her mother and Alexi the Miranda warning. Whatever info the two gave up could be used in a courtroom later.

Her mother twitched and looked over at Alexi as Troy's hands moved over her and up between her legs. "Can you please turn around?" Troy asked.

She turned around, and as their gazes met, there were tears pooling in her mother's eyes. "Baby," her mother began, "I'm so sorry about everything that happened. I didn't want anything to go this far."

The little flicker of hope Kate had been holding,

that her mother was innocent and Troy was wrong in assuming the worst, died.

Troy had been right.

"How was Sal involved?" She tried to sound confident, like she knew exactly what had happened and was simply waiting for an admission before arresting her mother.

"Your mother didn't do anything wrong," Alexi interrupted. "This was all my idea. Sal was on my payroll—he was working for me. But he was acting on his own in all of this. It wasn't our plan for him to shoot anyone. He went rogue."

That, right there, was enough of an admission to provide a valid reason to arrest and charge both Alexi and her mother with murder. And yet she hated the idea.

How had they gotten themselves into such a predicament? And how had she found herself holding the only sets of handcuffs?

"And what was he doing for you, exactly?" Kate asked.

"As you likely know, he was the engineering director at the company." Alexi sounded pathetic. "It started out as just a friendship, but he told me things… Things, about the projects we were working on, that others wanted to know."

Troy grimaced and motioned to Alexi's feet. "Spread them." He did a quick pat of Alexi and stepped back. "Which *others* wanted to know about your projects?"

"Well—" Alexi paused "—there were a couple of people. I don't know who they were with, but they were offering a hell of a lot of money. And…well… I make good change, but I could retire on what they promised. All they wanted were a few schematics. Nothing that could really compromise any sort of government project. It was just parts. You know? No big deal."

This was why the government had to use a variety of machining companies to do their work—small leaks like this.

"How much?" Troy asked.

"Fourteen million, all paid through Bitcoin," Alexi said, sounding a bit proud. "They started at five. Seriously, a little more time and I think I could have gotten them higher, but at what point do you just not need any more money, am I right?"

Kate's knees grew weaker as she listened to the terrible story unfold. There were so many things wrong that she couldn't find a silver lining. Her life was imploding around her.

And whether or not her mother and Alexi realized it, what they were doing was illegal. She'd let a lawyer sort out all the charges, but she could think of several, some with stiff penalties.

"You are not seriously gloating about how much money you made off Solomon's death." Troy's tone was nearly a growl, and she was grateful for it.

"Absolutely not. That's not what I meant." Alexi put his hands up in surrender. "There was nothing illegal about what I did. I was just trying to make some money. I wanted to start a new life, a life that your mother would love… In a way she had grown accustomed to." He looked over at her mother, and the gaze her mother gave him nearly made her sick.

There were many things illegal about what they had done, but she wasn't about to point it out to them—not when she had them both on the ropes and talking about their crimes. Right now, she needed them to feel safe so they would tell her everything. She needed to pretend to be their friend so she and the FBI could formulate a full case and prosecute them to the fullest extent of the law—mother or not.

"So, you were going to run away with this man?" She tried to check any emotions from seeping into her tone, but it was a struggle, thanks to all the hate and disgust she was feeling.

Her mother looked down at the hood of the car.

"Mom, I get that love happens. I get that you can't always make sense of the things that you feel, and you sure as hell can make some terrible decisions. But why?"

Tears ran down her mother's face. "Why what?" she choked out.

"Why did you have to have my father killed? Did he learn what you guys were up to? That Sal and Alexi were working together to sell governmental secrets?"

Her mother sobbed, sitting back down on the car and resting her chin on her chest. "We told you. His death wasn't planned."

"Then why, Mom, why?"

"It was never supposed to happen this way… When I told him I wanted to leave…he blew up at me. He threatened to take everything." She took out a handkerchief from her pocket and softly wiped at the tip of her nose. "I was fine with that. I was willing to accept losing it all. Your father was a good man. He helped me through the cancer, through everything. It would be a lie to say that I didn't still love him. I just was no longer *in love* with him."

Her mother looked to her as if she was asking for her forgiveness and understanding.

Though she didn't feel either, she gave her mother a nod, hoping she would keep talking. "Did you pull the trigger?"

"No," her mother said, violently shaking her head. "That was Sal. He'd found out what happened. About the divorce. That's when your father hired your friend there…" She motioned toward Troy. "When I didn't fight your father for a division of the assets, he started to look into things…wondering why. I think he had started to sniff out Alexi, but he wasn't entirely sure."

"Deborah, you need to stop talking." Alexi shook his head. "We are innocent in this. That's all they need to know."

Her mother shook her head. "No. Kate is my daughter. Agent or not, she deserves to know that I'm not a murderer. After this breaks in the news, who knows what the public or a jury will say. Right now is the only chance to give her my full side of the story."

Kate swallowed back the bile rising in her throat. Her mother was very likely going to go to a federal penitentiary for this, and yet all she wanted to do was keep her daughter's love...and keep her from thinking the worst of her.

The world was a screwed-up place. And what made it worse was the fact that she couldn't stop her mother from talking. It went against her oath as an agent. She was to serve and protect the innocent. And, in this case, she was going to protect her father's memory over her mother's future.

"So, why would Sal pull the trigger and kill Solomon?" Troy asked, taking the lead as though he could tell exactly how hurt Kate was and what kind of turmoil she was in.

"Sal knew you would uncover the truth, that we had been using code to divert secrets to our mystery contact. He knew all about STEALTH and the power you guys have to get into any place you need. He convinced us it was only a matter of time until we were going to get caught. Our plan was just to take the money we had been stashing away in the Cayman Islands and disappear. But then, one day, out of the blue, Solomon called Sal into his office." Her mother looked at the car. "Things went south."

"And what about me, Mom? Why did you have your guy try to take me out?"

Her mother's sobbing intensified, but Kate didn't

feel sorry for her… Instead, oddly, she didn't feel anything.

"I told him not to. I told him he could have a bigger share of the money. But he knew you were breathing down our necks. It was only a matter of time. After what happened… I wanted to turn ourselves in… It's why we were here today. But…"

"Your mother is taking blame where there is none. We didn't do anything illegal," Alexi countered.

He could believe whatever he wanted; his ass was going to jail.

"Why didn't you guys leave after the shooting?" she asked.

Her mother sobbed. "I couldn't. It hurt so bad. I had to honor your father's memory before I could make another move."

She shook her head, trying to make sense of everything. "I appreciate what you are saying, Mom. I do." She drew in a long breath, accepting what she was going to have to do. "And I know this isn't your fault—at least, not completely… But, unfortunately, I'm going to have to place you under arrest."

Slipping the cuffs on her mother's wrists would be one sensation she would never forget. And yet being true and dedicated to her job and the world that trusted her had to come before protecting a criminal—even one who was family.

Epilogue

Six months later, Troy held his hands over Kate's eyes as he led her up the stairs and to the front door of her house. "No peeking, okay?" he asked, taking out the keys she had given him for her home from his pocket. "Promise?"

She giggled, nodding. "What are you up to?"

"Birthday girl, don't you worry."

"Oh yeah, you telling me not to worry is definitely going to make me feel at ease," she teased.

"You know, if you are going to be snarky, I don't *have* to give you your birthday present. I could just give it to some poor, hapless bystander. At least they would appreciate it."

She did a little hop from foot to foot, revealing her excitement. "Come on. I know I'm going to love whatever you are doing, but you are killing me. Can you open the door any slower?"

He laughed. She looked so damn cute standing there in her down jacket, bundled up. She had always called him her iceman, but now, looking at her, she was the one who seemed to better fit the part.

"After everything that happened with your mom, with Alexi's and her convictions, I wanted to do something special. I know you've been through a lot."

Her little happy dance stopped and he wished he hadn't started his speech out like he had, but there was no going back in time.

"Anyhow, I want you to know how I feel about you. And though we've kind of talked about things— we haven't *talked about things*." He could feel her eyelashes batting against his palm as he spoke.

Reaching up to the door knocker, he tapped out a rhythm of dashes and dots.

"Is that...?" she said, giggling. "Do it again."

"But I thought you knew Morse code," he teased, doing it again.

She laughed and she pulled his hand away from her face. "I do... And I knew what you were asking the first time. But...I wanted to hear you ask it again."

"Are you going to answer me?" he asked, smiling as he dropped to one knee.

"Yes." She clasped her hands to her mouth as he pulled the blue box out of his pocket. He opened it, and inside the box was a princess-cut diamond solitaire. "Oh my... Yes, Grim. Yes."

He took the ring out of the box, gently slipping it on her finger. "I love you, Ms. Scot. Or would you prefer *Mrs. Spade*?"

She lifted her hand, looking at the ring. "If I'm going to be your wife, I want to be *your* wife and you're going to be *my* husband. A name doesn't matter to me." She threw her arms around his neck. "I love you, Grim."

A single tear twisted down his cheek. "I love you too, Mrs. Spade."

She hugged him tighter, finally letting him go. "Hey, why the big surprise entrance to my house?" she asked, tilting her head to the side.

"Oh yeah," he said with a laugh. He hadn't intended on asking her to marry him right there, right now...and he had nearly forgotten the rest of his plan. Everything was all screwed up, but at the same time, this proposal was just like them...imperfectly perfect, and he'd have it no other way. "Close your eyes."

She did as instructed, and he opened the door.

"You can look."

She gasped.

Inside, hanging from line after line, were a thousand white cranes—the first of which he had folded for her while waiting for her in the coffee shop. Here was hoping the one thing he wished for above all others, the wish he had wished with every fold of the paper, would come true...the wish that they would be each other's forever.

* * * * *

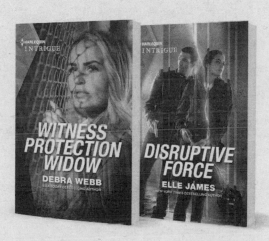

"I don't know anything," she said. "Why does TDC think I do?"

"I don't know." Was this an especially bold gambit on TDC's part, or merely a desperate one?

"Maybe this isn't about what TDC wants you to reveal," he said. "Maybe it's about what they think you know that they don't want you to say."

She pushed her hair back from her forehead, a distracted gesture. "I don't understand what you're getting at."

"Everything TDC is doing—the charges against your father, the big reward, the publicity—those are the actions of an organization that is desperate to find your father."

"Because they want to stop him from talking?"

"I could be wrong, but I think so."

Most of the color had left her face, but she remained strong. "That sounds dangerous," she said. "A lot more dangerous than diapers."

"You don't have any idea what TDC might be worried about?" he asked. "It could even be something your father mentioned to you in passing."

"He didn't talk to me about his work. He knew I wasn't interested."

"What did you talk about?" Maybe the answer lay there.

"What I was doing. What was going on in my life." She shrugged. "Sometimes we talked about music, or movies, or books. Travel—that was something we both enjoyed. There was nothing secret or mysterious or having anything to do with TDC."

"If you think of anything else, call me." It was what he always said to people involved in cases, but he hoped she really would call him.

"I will." Did he detect annoyance in her voice?

"What will you do about the lawsuit?" he asked.

She looked down at the white envelope. "I'll contact my attorney. The whole thing is ridiculous. And annoying." She shifted her gaze to him at the last word. Maybe a signal for him to go.

"I'll let you know if I hear any news," he said, moving toward the door.

"Thanks."

"Try not to worry," he said. Then he added, "I'll protect you." Because it was the right thing to say. Because it was his job.

Because he realized nothing was more important to him at this moment.

Don't miss
Mountain Investigation *by Cindi Myers,*
available March 2021 wherever
Harlequin Intrigue books and ebooks are sold.

Harlequin.com

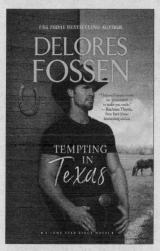

Love Harlequin romance?

DISCOVER.

Be the first to find out about promotions, news and exclusive content!

Facebook.com/HarlequinBooks

Twitter.com/HarlequinBooks

Instagram.com/HarlequinBooks

Pinterest.com/HarlequinBooks

ReaderService.com

EXPLORE.

Sign up for the Harlequin e-newsletter and download a free book from any series at **TryHarlequin.com**

CONNECT.

Join our Harlequin community to share your thoughts and connect with other romance readers!
Facebook.com/groups/HarlequinConnection

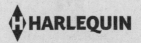